THE NEW WINDMILL SERIES
General Editors: Anne and Ian Serraillier

56

THE RED PONY

JOHN STEINBECK

The Red Pony

ILLUSTRATED BY

ROBERT HODGSON

HEINEMANN EDUCATIONAL BOOKS

LONDON

Heinemann Educational Books Ltd
22 Bedford Square, London WC1B 3HH

LONDON   EDINBURGH   MELBOURNE   AUCKLAND
SINGAPORE   KUALA LUMPUR   NEW DELHI
IBADAN   NAIROBI   JOHANNESBURG
PORTSMOUTH (NH)   KINGSTON

ISBN 0 435 12056 5

First published by William Heinemann Ltd 1938
First published in the New Windmill Series 1961
Reprinted 1962, 1963, 1965, 1967, 1968, 1969,
1970, 1972, 1973, 1975, 1977, 1978,
1982, 1984, 1985, 1986, 1988

Printed and bound in Great Britain by
Richard Clay Ltd, Bungay, Suffolk

I

The
Gift

At daybreak Billy Buck emerged from the bunk-house and stood for a moment on the porch looking up at the sky. He was a broad, bandy-legged little man with a walrus moustache, with square hands, puffed and muscled on the palms. His eyes were a contemplative, watery grey and the hair which protruded from under his Stetson hat was spiky and weathered. Billy was still stuffing his shirt into his blue jeans as he stood on the porch. He unbuckled his belt and tightened it again. The belt showed, by the worn

shiny places opposite each hole, the gradual increase of
Billy's middle over a period of years. When he had seen
to the weather, Billy cleared each nostril by holding its
mate closed with his forefinger and blowing fiercely.
Then he walked down to the barn, rubbing his hands
together. He curried and brushed two saddle horses in
the stalls, talking quietly to them all the time; and he had
hardly finished when the iron triangle started ringing at
the ranch-house. Billy stuck the brush and currycomb
together and laid them on the rail and went up to breakfast. His action had been so deliberate and yet so waste-
less of time that he came to the house while Mrs Tiflin
was still ringing the triangle. She nodded her grey head
to him and withdrew into the kitchen. Billy Buck sat
down on the steps, because he was a cow-hand, and it
wouldn't be fitting that he should go first into the dining-
room. He heard Mr Tiflin in the house, stamping his
feet into his boots.

The high jangling note of the triangle put the boy
Jody in motion. He was only a little boy, ten years old,
with hair like dusty yellow grass and with shy polite grey
eyes, and with a mouth that worked when he thought.
The triangle picked him up out of sleep. It didn't occur
to him to disobey the harsh note. He never had; no one
he knew ever had. He brushed the tangled hair out of
his eyes and skinned his nightgown off. In a moment he
was dressed – blue chambray shirt and overalls. It was
late in the summer, so of course there were no shoes to
bother with. In the kitchen he waited until his mother

got from in front of the sink and went back to the stove. Then he washed himself and brushed back his wet hair with his fingers. His mother turned sharply on him as he left the sink. Jody looked shyly away.

'I've got to cut your hair before long,' his mother said. 'Breakfast's on the table. Go on in, so Billy can come.'

Jody sat at the long table which was covered with white oilcloth washed through to the fabric in some places. The fried eggs lay in rows on their platter. Jody took three eggs on his plate and followed with three thick slices of crisp bacon. He carefully scraped a spot of blood from one of the egg yolks.

Billy Buck clumped in. 'That won't hurt you,' Billy explained. 'That's only a sign the rooster leaves.'

Jody's tall stern father came in then and Jody knew from the noise on the floor that he was wearing boots, but he looked under the table anyway, to make sure. His father turned off the oil lamp over the table, for plenty of morning light now came through the windows.

Jody did not ask where his father and Billy Buck were riding that day, but he wished he might go along. His father was a disciplinarian. Jody obeyed him in everything without questions of any kind. Now Carl Tiflin sat down and reached for the egg platter.

'Got the cows ready to go, Billy?' he asked.

'In the lower corral,' Billy said. 'I could just as well take them in alone.'

'Sure you could. But a man needs company. Besides,

your throat gets pretty dry.' Carl Tiflin was jovial this morning.

Jody's mother put her head in the door. 'What time do you think to be back, Carl?'

'I can't tell. I've got to see some men in Salinas. Might be gone till dark.'

The eggs and coffee and big biscuits disappeared rapidly. Jody followed the two men out of the house. He watched them mount their horses and drive six old milk cows out of the corral and start over the hill toward Salinas. They were going to sell the old cows to the butcher.

When they had disappeared over the crown of the ridge Jody walked up the hill behind the house. The dogs trotted around the house corner hunching their shoulders and grinning horribly with pleasure. Jody patted their heads – Doubletree Mutt with the big thick tail and yellow eyes, and Smasher, the shepherd, who had killed a coyote and lost an ear doing it. Smasher's one good ear stood up higher than a collie's ear should. Billy Buck said that always happened. After the frenzied greeting the dogs lowered their noses to the ground in a business-like way and went ahead, looking back now and then to make sure that the boy was coming. They walked up through the chicken-yard and saw the quail eating with the chickens. Smasher chased the chickens a little to keep in practice in case there should ever be sheep to herd. Jody continued on through the large vegetable patch where the green corn was higher than his head.

The cow-pumpkins were green and small yet. He went on to the sagebrush line where the cold spring ran out of its pipe and fell into a round wooden tub. He leaned over and drank close to the green mossy wood where the water tasted best. Then he turned and looked back on the ranch, on the low, whitewashed house girded with red geraniums, and on the long bunk-house by the cypress tree where Billy Buck lived alone. Jody could see the great black kettle under the cypress tree. That was where the pigs were scalded. The sun was coming over the ridge now, glaring on the whitewash of the houses and barns, making the wet grass blaze softly. Behind him, in the tall sagebrush, the birds were scampering on the ground, making a great noise among the dry leaves; the squirrels piped shrilly on the side-hills. Jody looked along at the farm buildings. He felt an uncertainty in the air, a feeling of change and of loss and of the gain of new and unfamiliar things. Over the hillside two big black buzzards sailed low to the ground and their shadows slipped smoothly and quickly ahead of them. Some animal had died in the vicinity. Jody knew it. It might be a cow or it might be the remains of a rabbit. The buzzards overlooked nothing. Jody hated them as all decent things hate them, but they could not be hurt because they made away with carrion.

After a while the boy sauntered downhill again. The dogs had long ago given him up and gone into the brush to do things in their own way. Back through the vegetable garden he went, and he paused for a moment to smash a green musk-melon with his heel, but he was not happy about it. It was a bad thing to do, he knew perfectly well. He kicked dirt over the ruined melon to conceal it.

Back at the house his mother bent over his rough hands, inspecting his fingers and nails. It did little good to start him clean to school, for too many things could happen on the way. She sighed over the black cracks on his fingers, and then gave him his books and his lunch and started him on the mile walk to school. She noticed that his mouth was working a good deal this morning.

Jody started his journey. He filled his pockets with little pieces of white quartz that lay in the road, and every so often he took a shot at a bird or at some rabbit that had stayed sunning itself in the road too long. At the crossroads over the bridge he met two friends and the three of them walked to school together, making ridiculous strides and being rather silly. School had just opened two weeks before. There was still a spirit of revolt among the pupils.

It was four o'clock in the afternoon when Jody topped the hill and looked down on the ranch again. He looked for the saddle horses, but the corral was empty. His father was not back yet. He went slowly then toward the afternoon chores. At the ranch-house he found his mother sitting on the porch, mending socks.

'There's two doughnuts in the kitchen for you,' she said. Jody slid to the kitchen, and returned with half of one of the doughnuts already eaten and his mouth full.

His mother asked him what he had learned in school that day, but she didn't listen to his doughnut-muffled answer. She interrupted: 'Jody, to-night see you fill the wood-box clear full. Last night you crossed the sticks and it wasn't only about half full. Lay the sticks flat to-night. And Jody, some of the hens are hiding eggs, or else the dogs are eating them. Look about in the grass and see if you can find any nests.'

Jody, still eating, went out and did his chores. He saw the quail come down to eat with the chickens when he threw out the grain. For some reason his father was proud to have them come. He never allowed any shooting near the house for fear the quail might go away.

When the wood-box was full, Jody took his twenty-two rifle up to the cold spring at the brush line. He drank again and then aimed the gun at all manner of things, at rocks, at birds on the wing, at the big black pig kettle under the cypress tree, but he didn't shoot, for he had no cartridges and wouldn't have until he was twelve. If his father had seen him aim the rifle in the direction of the house he would have put the cartridges off another year. Jody remembered this and did not point the rifle down the hill again. Two years was enough to wait for cartridges. Nearly all of his father's presents were given with reservations which hampered their value somewhat. It was good discipline.

The supper waited until dark for his father to return. When at last he came in with Billy Buck, Jody could smell the delicious brandy on their breaths. Inwardly he rejoiced, for his father sometimes talked to him when he smelled of brandy, sometimes even told things he had done in the wild days when he was a boy.

After supper Jody sat by the fireplace and his shy polite eyes sought the room corners, and he waited for his father to tell what it was he contained, for Jody knew he had news of some sort. But he was disappointed. His father pointed a stern finger at him.

'You'd better go to bed, Jody. I'm going to need you in the morning.'

That wasn't so bad. Jody liked to do the things he had to do as long as they weren't routine things. He looked at the floor and his mouth worked out a question before he spoke it. 'What are we going to do in the morning, kill a pig?' he asked softly.

'Never you mind. You better get to bed.'

When the door was closed behind him, Jody heard his father and Billy Buck chuckling and he knew it was a joke of some kind. And later, when he lay in bed, trying to make words out of the murmurs in the other room, he heard his father protest, 'But, Ruth, I didn't give much for him.'

Jody heard the hoot-owls hunting mice down by the barn, and he heard a fruit-tree limb tap-tapping against the house. A cow was lowing when he went to sleep.

When the triangle sounded in the morning, Jody dressed more quickly even than usual. In the kitchen, while he washed his face and combed back his hair, his mother addressed him irritably. 'Don't you go out until you get a good breakfast in you.'

He went into the dining-room and sat at the long white table. He took a steaming hotcake from the platter, arranged two fried eggs on it, covered them with another hotcake and squashed the whole thing with his fork.

His father and Billy Buck came in. Jody knew from the sound on the floor that both of them were wearing flat-heeled shoes, but he peered under the table to make sure. His father turned off the oil lamp, for the day had arrived, and he looked stern and disciplinary, but Billy Buck didn't look at Jody at all. He avoided the shy questioning eyes of the boy and soaked a whole piece of toast in his coffee.

Carl Tiflin said crossly, 'You come with us after breakfast!'

Jody had trouble with his food then, for he felt a kind of doom in the air. After Billy had tilted his saucer and drained the coffee which had slopped into it, and had wiped his hands on his jeans, the two men stood up from the table and went out into the morning light together, and Jody respectfully followed a little behind them. He tried to keep his mind from running ahead, tried to keep it absolutely motionless.

His mother called, 'Carl! Don't you let it keep him from school.'

They marched past the cypress, where a single tree hung from a limb to butcher the pigs on, and past the black iron kettle, so it was not a pig-killing. The sun shone over the hill and threw long, dark shadows of the trees and buildings. They crossed a stubble-field to short-cut to the barn. Jody's father unhooked the door and they went in. They had been walking toward the sun on the way down. The barn was black as night in contrast and warm from the hay and from the beasts. Jody's father moved over toward the one box stall. 'Come here!' he ordered. Jody could begin to see things now. He looked into the box stall and then stepped back quickly.

A red pony colt was looking at him out of the stall. Its tense ears were forward and a light of disobedience was in its eyes. Its coat was rough and thick as an Airedale's fur and its mane was long and tangled. Jody's throat collapsed in on itself and cut his breath short.

'He needs a good currying,' his father said, 'and if I ever hear of you not feeding him or leaving his stall dirty, I'll sell him off in a minute.'

Jody couldn't bear to look at the pony's eyes any more. He gazed down at his hands for a moment, and he asked very shyly: 'Mine?' No one answered him. He put his hand out toward the pony. Its grey nose came close, sniffing loudly, and then the lips drew back and the strong teeth closed on Jody's fingers. The pony shook its head up and down and seemed to laugh with amuse-ment. Jody regarded his bruised fingers. 'Well,' he said with pride – 'well, I guess he can bite all right.' The two men laughed, somewhat in relief. Carl Tiflin went out of the barn and walked up a side-hill to be by himself, for he was embarrassed, but Billy Buck stayed. It was easier to talk to Billy Buck. Jody asked again – 'Mine?'

Billy became professional in tone. 'Sure! That is, if you look out for him and break him right. I'll show you how. He's just a colt. You can't ride him for some time.'

Jody put out his bruised hand again, and this time the red pony let his nose be rubbed. 'It ought to have a carrot,' Jody said. 'Where'd we get him, Billy?'

'Bought him at a sheriff's auction,' Billy explained. 'A show went broke in Salinas and had debts. The sheriff was selling off their stuff.'

The pony stretched out his nose and shook the forelock from his wild eyes. Jody stroked the nose a little. He said softly, 'There isn't a – saddle?'

Billy Buck laughed. 'I'd forgot. Come along.'

In the harness-room he lifted down a little saddle of red morocco leather. 'It's just a show saddle,' Billy Buck said disparagingly. 'It isn't practical for the brush, but it was cheap at the sale.'

Jody couldn't trust himself to look at the saddle either, and he couldn't speak at all. He brushed the shining red leather with his finger-tips, and after a long while he said, 'It'll look pretty on him, though.' He thought of the grandest and prettiest things he knew. 'If he hasn't a name already, I think I'll call him Gabilan Mountains,' he said.

Billy Buck knew how he felt. 'It's a pretty long name. Why don't you call him Gabilan? That means hawk. That would be a fine name for him.' Billy felt glad. 'If you will collect tail hair, I might be able to make a hair rope for you sometime. You could use it for a hacka-more.'[1]

Jody wanted to go back to the box stall. 'Could I lead him to school, do you think – to show the kids?'

But Billy shook his head. 'He's not even halter-broke yet. We had a time getting him here. Had to almost drag him. You better be starting for school, though.'

'I'll bring the kids to see him here this afternoon,' Jody said.

Six boys came over the hill half an hour early that afternoon, running hard, their heads down, their fore-arms working, their breath whistling. They swept by the house and cut across the stubble-field to the barn. And then they stood self-consciously before the pony, and then they looked at Jody with eyes in which there was a new admiration and a new respect. Before to-day Jody had been a boy, dressed in overalls and a blue shirt – quieter than most, even suspected of being a little cowardly. And now he was different. Out of a thousand centuries they drew the ancient admiration of the foot-man for the horseman. They knew instinctively that a man on a horse is spiritually as well as physically bigger than a man on foot. They knew that Jody had been miraculously lifted out of equality with them, and had been placed over them. Gabilan put his head out of the stall and sniffed them.

1. Halter made of horsehair.

'Why'n't you ride him?' the boys cried. 'Why'n't you braid his tail with ribbons like in the fair?' 'When you going to ride him?'

Jody's courage was up. He too felt the superiority of the horseman. 'He's not old enough. Nobody can ride him for a long time. I'm going to train him on the long halter. Billy Buck is going to show me how.'

'Well, can't we even lead him around a little?'

'He isn't even halter-broke,' Jody said. He wanted to be completely alone when he took the pony out for the first time. 'Come and see the saddle.'

They were speechless at the red morocco saddle, completely shocked out of comment. 'It isn't much use in the brush.' Jody explained. 'It'll look pretty on him, though. Maybe I'll ride bareback when I go into the brush.'

'How you going to rope a cow without a saddle horn?'

'Maybe I'll get another saddle for every day. My father might want me to help him with the stock.' He let them feel the red saddle, and showed them the brass chain throat-latch on the bridle and the big brass buttons at each temple where the headstall and brow band crossed. The whole thing was too wonderful. They had to go away after a little while, and each boy, in his mind, searched among his possessions for a bribe worthy of offering in return for a ride on the red pony when the time should come.

Jody was glad when they had gone. He took brush and curry-comb from the wall, took down the barrier of the box stall and stepped cautiously in. The pony's eyes glittered, and he edged around into kicking position. But Jody touched him on the shoulder and rubbed his high arched neck as he had always seen Billy Buck do, and he crooned, 'So-o-o, Boy,' in a deep voice. The pony gradually relaxed his tenseness. Jody curried and brushed until a pile of dead hair lay in the stall and until the pony's coat had taken on a deep red shine. Each time he finished he thought it might have been done better. He braided the mane into a dozen little pigtails, and he braided the forelock, and then he undid them and brushed the hair out straight again.

Jody did not hear his mother enter the barn. She was angry when she came, but when she looked in at the pony and at Jody working over him, she felt a curious pride rise up in her. 'Have you forgot the wood-box?' she asked gently. 'It's not far off from dark and there's not a stick of wood in the house, and the chickens aren't fed.'

Jody quickly put up his tools. 'I forgot, ma'am.'

'Well, after this do your chores first. Then you won't forget. I expect you'll forget lots of things now if I don't keep an eye on you.'

'Can I have carrots from the garden for him, ma'am?'

She had to think about that. 'Oh – I guess so, if you only take the big tough ones.'

'Carrots keep the coat good,' he said, and again she felt the curious rush of pride.

Jody never waited for the triangle to get him out of

bed after the coming of the pony. It became his habit to creep out of bed even before his mother was awake, to slip into his clothes and to go quietly down to the barn to see Gabilan. In the grey quiet mornings when the land and the brush and the houses and the trees were silver-grey and black like a photograph negative, he stole toward the barn, past the sleeping stones and the sleeping cypress tree. The turkeys, roosting in the tree out of coyotes' reach, clicked drowsily. The fields glowed with a grey frost-like light and in the dew the tracks of rabbits and of fieldmice stood out sharply. The good dogs came stiffly out of their little houses, hackles up and deep growls in their throats. Then they caught Jody's scent, and their stiff tails rose up and waved a greeting – Doubletree Mutt with the big thick tail, and Smasher, the incipient shepherd – then went lazily back to their warm beds.

It was a strange time and a mysterious journey, to Jody – an extension of a dream. When he first had the pony he liked to torture himself during the trip by thinking Gabilan would not be in his stall, and worse, would never have been there. And he had other delicious little self-induced pains. He thought how the rats had gnawed ragged holes in the red saddle, and how the mice had nibbled Gabilan's tail until it was stringy and thin. He usually ran the last little way to the barn. He unlatched the rusty hasp of the barn door and stepped in, and, no matter how quietly he opened the door, Gabilan was always looking at him over the barrier of the box stall and Gabilan whinnied softly and stamped his front foot, and his eyes had big sparks of red fire in them like oakwood embers.

Sometimes, if the work-horses were to be used that day, Jody found Billy Buck in the barn harnessing and currying. Billy stood with him and looked long at Gabilan and he told Jody a great many things about horses. He explained that they were terribly afraid for their feet, so that one must make a practice of lifting the legs and patting the hooves and ankles to remove their terror. He told Jody how horses love conversation. He must talk to the pony all the time, and tell him the reasons for everything. Billy wasn't sure a horse could understand everything that was said to him, but it was impossible to say how much was understood. A horse never kicked up a fuss if someone he liked explained things to him. Billy could give examples, too. He had known, for instance, a horse nearly dead-beat with fatigue to perk up when told it was only a little farther to his destination. And he had known a horse paralysed with fright to come out of it when his rider told him what it was that was frightening him. While he talked in the mornings, Billy Buck cut twenty or thirty straws into neat three-inch lengths and stuck them into his hat-band. Then, during the whole day, if he wanted to pick his teeth or merely to chew on something, he had only to reach up for one of them.

Jody listened carefully, for he knew and the whole country knew that Billy Buck was a fine hand with horses. Billy's own horse was a stringy cayuse[1] with a hammer head, but he nearly always won the first prizes at the stock trials. Billy could rope a steer, take a double half-hitch about the horn with his riata,[2] and dismount, and his horse would play the steer as an angler plays a fish, keeping a tight rope until the steer was down or beaten.

Every morning, after Jody had curried and brushed the pony, he let down the barrier of the stall, and Gabilan thrust past him and raced down the barn and into the corral. Around and around he galloped, and sometimes he jumped forward and landed on stiff legs. He stood quivering, stiff ears forward, eyes rolling so that the whites showed, pretending to be frightened. At last he walked snorting to the water-trough and buried his nose in the water up to the nostrils. Jody was proud then, for he knew that was the way to judge a horse. Poor horses only touched their lips to the water, but a fine spirited beast put his whole nose and mouth under, and only left room to breathe.

Then Jody stood and watched the pony, and he saw things he had never noticed about any other horse, the sleek, sliding flank muscles and the cords of the buttocks, which flexed like a closing fist, and the shine the sun put on the red coat. Having seen horses all his life, Jody had never looked at them very closely before. But now he noticed the moving ears, which gave expression and even

1. Indian pony.
2. Lariat, lasso.

inflection of expression to the face. The pony talked with his ears. You could tell exactly how he felt about everything by the way his ears pointed. Sometimes they were stiff and upright and sometimes lax and sagging. They went back when he was angry or fearful, and forward when he was anxious and curious and pleased; and their exact position indicated which emotion he had.

Billy Buck kept his word. In the early fall[1] the training began. First there was the halter-breaking, and that was the hardest because it was the first thing. Jody held a carrot and coaxed and promised and pulled on the rope. The pony set his feet like a burro[2] when he felt the strain. But before long he learned. Jody walked all over the ranch leading him. Gradually he took to dropping the rope until the pony followed him unled wherever he went.

And then came the training on the long halter. That was slower work. Jody stood in the middle of the circle, holding the long halter. He clucked with his tongue and the pony started to walk in a big circle, held in by the long rope. He clucked again to make the pony trot, and again to make him gallop. Around and around Gabilan went thundering and enjoying it immensely. Then he called 'Whoa', and the pony stopped. It was not long until Gabilan was perfect at it. But in many ways he was a bad pony. He bit Jody in the legs and stomped on Jody's feet. Now and then his ears went back and he aimed a tremendous kick at the boy. Every time he did one of these bad things, Gabilan settled back and seemed

1. Autumn.   2. Donkey.

to laugh at himself.

Billy Buck worked at the hair rope in the evenings before the fireplace. Jody collected tail hair in a bag, and he sat and watched Billy slowly constructing the rope, twisting a few hairs to make a string and rolling two strings together for a cord, and then braiding a number of cords to make the rope. Billy rolled the finished rope on the floor under his foot to make it round and hard.

The long halter work rapidly approached perfection. Jody's father, watching the pony stop and start and trot and gallop, was a little bothered by it.

'He's getting to be almost a trick pony,' he complained. 'I don't like trick horses. It takes all the – dignity out of a horse to make him do tricks. Why, a trick horse is kind of like an actor – no dignity, no character of his own.' And his father said, 'I guess you better be getting him used to the saddle pretty soon.'

Jody rushed for the harness-room. For some time he had been riding the saddle on a saw-horse.[1] He changed the stirrup length over and over, and could never get it just right. Sometimes, mounted on the saw-horse in the harness-room, with collars and hames[2] and tugs[3] hung all about him, Jody rode out beyond the room. He carried his rifle across the pommel. He saw the fields go

1. Frame on which wood is sawn.
2. Two curved pieces of wood attached to the collar of a draught horse.
3. Pair of short chains attached to the hames, by which the collar is connected with the shafts.

flying by, and he heard the beat of the galloping hoofs.

It was a ticklish job, saddling the pony the first time. Gabilan hunched and reared and threw the saddle off before the cinch[1] could be tightened. It had to be replaced again and again until at last the pony let it stay. And the cinching was difficult, too. Day by day Jody tightened the girth a little more until at last the pony didn't mind the saddle at all.

Then there was the bridle. Billy explained how to use a stick of licorice for a bit until Gabilan was used to having something in his mouth. Billy explained, 'Of course we could force-break him to everything, but he wouldn't be as good a horse if we did. He'd always be a little bit afraid, and he wouldn't mind because he wanted to.'

The first time the pony wore the bridle he whipped his head about and worked his tongue against the bit until the blood oozed from the corners of his mouth. He tried to rub the headstall off on the manger. His ears pivoted about and his eyes turned red with fear and with general devilishness. Jody rejoiced, for he knew that only a mean-souled horse does not resent training.

And Jody trembled when he thought of the time when he would first sit in the saddle. The pony would probably throw him off. There was no disgrace in that. The disgrace would come if he did not get right up and mount again. Sometimes he dreamed that he lay in the dirt and cried and couldn't make himself mount again.

1. Saddle-girth.

The shame of the dream lasted until the middle of the day.

Gabilan was growing fast. Already he had lost the long-leggedness of the colt; his mane was getting longer and blacker. Under the constant currying and brushing his coat lay as smooth and gleaming as orange-red lacquer. Jody oiled the hoofs and kept them carefully trimmed so they would not crack.

The hair rope was nearly finished. Jody's father gave him an old pair of spurs and bent in the side bars and cut down the strap and took up the chainlets until they fitted. And then one day Carl Tiflin said:

'The pony's growing faster than I thought. I guess you can ride him by Thanksgiving. Think you can stick on?'

'I don't know,' said Jody shyly. Thanksgiving was only three weeks off. He hoped it wouldn't rain, for rain would spot the red saddle.

Gabilan knew and liked Jody by now. He nickered when Jody came across the stubble-field, and in the pasture he came running when his master whistled for him. There was always a carrot for him every time.

Billy Buck gave him riding instructions over and over. 'Now when you get up there, just grab tight with your knees and keep your hands away from the saddle, and if you get throwed, don't let that stop you. No matter how good a man is, there's always some horse can pitch him. You just climb up again before he gets to feeling smart about it. Pretty soon, he won't throw you no more, and pretty soon he can't throw you no more. That's the way to do it.'

'I hope it don't rain before,' Jody said.

Why not? Don't want to get throwed in the mud?'

That was partly it, and also he was afraid that in the flurry of bucking Gabilan might slip and fall on him and break his leg or his hip. He had seen that happen to men before, had seen how they writhed on the ground like squashed bugs, and he was afraid of it.

He practised on the saw-horse how he would hold the reins in his left hand and a hat in his right hand. If he kept his hands thus busy, he couldn't grab the horn if he felt himself going off. He didn't like to think of what would happen if he did grab the horn. Perhaps his father and Billy Buck would never speak to him again, they would be so ashamed. The news would get about and his mother would be ashamed too. And in the school yard – it was too awful to contemplate.

He began putting his weight in a stirrup when Gabilan was saddled, but he didn't throw his leg over the pony's back. That was forbidden until Thanksgiving.

Every afternoon he put the red saddle on the pony and cinched it tight. The pony was learning already to fill his stomach out unnaturally large while the cinching was going on, and then to let it down when the straps were fixed. Sometimes Jody led him up to the brush line and let him drink from the round green tub, and some-times he led him up through the stubble-field to the hilltop from which it was possible to see the white town of Salinas and the geometric fields of the great valley, and the oak trees clipped by the sheep. Now and then they broke through the brush and came to little cleared circles so hedged in that the world was gone and only the sky and the circle of brush were left from the old life. Gabilan liked these trips and showed it by keeping his head very high and by quivering his nostrils with interest. When the two came back from an expedition they smelled of the sweet sage they had forced through.

Time dragged on toward Thanksgiving, but winter came fast. The clouds swept down and hung all day over the land and brushed the hilltops, and the winds blew shrilly at night. All day the dry oak-leaves drifted down from the trees until they covered the ground, and yet the trees were unchanged.

Jody had wished it might not rain before Thanksgiving, but it did. The brown earth turned dark and the trees glistened. The cut ends of the stubble turned black with mildew; the haystacks greyed from exposure to the damp, and on the roofs the moss, which had been all summer as grey as lizards, turned a brilliant yellow-green. During the week of rain Jody kept the pony in the box stall out of the dampness, except for a little time after school when he took him out for exercise and to drink at the water-trough in the upper corral. Not once did Gabilan get wet.

The wet weather continued until little new grass

appeared. Jody walked to school dressed in a slicker[1] and short rubber boots. At length one morning the sun came out brightly. Jody, at his work in the box stall, said to Billy Buck, 'Maybe I'll leave Gabilan in the corral when I go to school to-day.'

'Be good for him out in the sun,' Billy assured him. 'No animal likes to be cooped up too long. Your father and me are going back on the hill to clean the leaves out of the spring.' Billy nodded and picked his teeth with one of his little straws.

'If the rain comes, though –' Jody suggested.

'Not likely to rain to-day. She's rained herself out.' Billy pulled up his sleeves and snapped his arm bands. 'If it comes on to rain – why, a little rain don't hurt a horse.'

'Well, if it does come on to rain, you put him in, will you, Billy? I'm scared he might get cold so I couldn't ride him when the time comes.'

'Oh, sure! I'll watch out for him if we get back in time. But it won't rain to-day.'

And so Jody, when he went to school, left Gabilan standing out in the corral.

Billy Buck wasn't wrong about many things. He couldn't be. But he was wrong about the weather that day, for a little after noon the clouds pushed over the hills and the rain began to pour down. Jody heard it start on the school-house roof. He considered holding up one finger for permission to go to the outhouse and, once

1. Waterproof coat.

outside, running for home to put the pony in. Punishment would be prompt both at school and at home. He gave it up and took ease from Billy's assurance that rain couldn't hurt a horse. When school was finally out, he hurried home through the dark rain. The banks at the sides of the road spouted little jets of muddy water. The rain slanted and swirled under a cold and gusty wind. Jody dog-trotted home, slopping through the gravelly mud of the road.

From the top of the ridge he could see Gabilan standing miserably in the corral. The red coat was almost black, and streaked with water. He stood head down with his rump to the rain and wind. Jody arrived running and threw open the barn door and led the wet pony in by his forelock. Then he found a gunny sack and rubbed the soaked hair and rubbed the legs and ankles. Gabilan stood patiently, but he trembled in gusts like the wind.

When he had dried the pony as well as he could, Jody went up to the house and brought hot water down to the barn and soaked the grain in it. Gabilan was not very hungry. He nibbled at the hot mash, but he was not very much interested in it, and he still shivered now and then. A little steam rose from his damp back.

It was almost dark when Billy Buck and Carl Tiflin came home. 'When the rain started we put up at Ben Herche's place, and the rain never let up all afternoon,' Carl Tiflin explained. Jody looked reproachfully at Billy Buck and Billy felt guilty.

'You said it wouldn't rain,' Jody accused him.

Billy looked away. 'It's hard to tell, this time of year,' he said, but his excuse was lame. He had no right to be fallible, and he knew it.

'The pony got wet, got soaked through.'

'Did you dry him off?'

'I rubbed him with a sack and I gave him hot grain.' Billy nodded in agreement.

'Do you think he'll take cold, Billy?'

'A little rain never hurt anything,' Billy assured him.

Jody's father joined the conversation then and lectured the boy a little. 'A horse,' he said, 'isn't any lap-dog kind of thing.' Carl Tiflin hated weakness and sickness, and he held a violent contempt for helplessness.

Jody's mother put a platter of steaks on the table and boiled potatoes and boiled squash, which clouded the room with their steam. They sat down to eat. Carl Tiflin still grumbled about weakness put into animals and men by too much coddling.

Billy Buck felt bad about his mistake. 'Did you blanket him?' he asked.

'No. I couldn't find any blanket. I laid some sacks over his back.'

'We'll go down and cover him up after we eat, then.' Billy felt better about it then. When Jody's father had gone in to the fire and his mother was washing dishes, Billy found and lighted a lantern. He and Jody walked through the mud to the barn. The barn was dark and warm and sweet. The horses still munched their evening

hay. 'You hold the lantern!' Billy ordered. And he felt
the pony's legs and tested the heat of the flanks. He put
his cheek against the pony's grey muzzle and then he
rolled up the eyelids to look at the eyeballs and he lifted
the lips to see the gums, and he put his fingers inside the
ears. 'He don't seem so chipper,' Billy said. 'I'll give him
a rub-down.'

Then Billy found a sack and rubbed the pony's legs
violently and he rubbed the chest and the withers.
Gabilan was strangely spiritless. He submitted patiently
to the rubbing. At last Billy brought an old cotton com-
forter[1] from the saddle-room, and threw it over the pony's
back and tied it at neck and chest with string.

'Now he'll be all right in the morning,' Billy said.

Jody's mother looked up when he got back to the
house. 'You're late up from bed,' she said. She held his
chin in her hard hand and brushed the tangled hair out
of his eyes and she said, 'Don't worry about the pony.
He'll be all right. Billy's as good as any horse-doctor in
the country.'

Jody hadn't known she could see his worry. He pulled
gently away from her and knelt down in front of the
fireplace until it burned his stomach. He scorched himself through and then went in to bed, but it was a hard
thing to go to sleep. He awakened after what seemed a
long time. The room was dark, but there was a greyness
in the window like that which precedes the dawn. He

1. Bedspread.

got up and found his overalls and searched for the legs, and then the clock in the other room struck two. He laid his clothes down and got back into bed. It was broad daylight when he awakened again. For the first time he had slept through the ringing of the triangle. He leaped up, flung on his clothes and went out of the door still buttoning his shirt. His mother looked after him for a moment and then went quietly back to her work. Her eyes were brooding and kind. Now and then her mouth smiled a little, but without changing her eyes at all.

Jody ran on toward the barn. Halfway there he heard the sound he dreaded, the hollow rasping cough of a horse. He broke into a sprint then. In the barn he found Billy Buck with the pony. Billy was rubbing its legs with his strong, thick hands. He looked up and smiled gaily. 'He just took a little cold,' Billy said. 'We'll have him out of it in a couple of days.'

Jody looked at the pony's face. The eyes were half closed and the lids thick and dry. In the eye corners a crust of hard mucus stuck. Gabilan's ears hung loosely sideways and his head was low. Jody put out his hand, but the pony did not move close to it. He coughed again and his whole body constricted with the effort. A little stream of thin fluid ran from his nostrils.

Jody looked back at Billy Buck. 'He's awful sick, Billy.'

'Just a little cold, like I said,' Billy insisted. 'You go get some breakfast and then go back to school. I'll take care of him.'

'But you might have to do something else. You might leave him.'

'No, I won't. I won't leave him at all. To-morrow's Saturday. Then you can stay with him all day.' Billy had failed again, and he felt badly about it. He had to cure the pony now.

Jody walked up to the house and took his place listlessly at the table. The eggs and bacon were cold and greasy, but he didn't notice it. He ate his usual amount. He didn't even ask to stay home from school. His mother pushed his hair back when she took his plate. 'Billy'll take care of the pony,' she assured him.

He moped through the whole day at school. He couldn't answer any questions nor read any words. He couldn't even tell anyone the pony was sick, for that might make him sicker. And when school was finally out he started home in dread. He walked slowly and let the other boys leave him. He wished he might continue walking and never arrive at the ranch.

Billy was in the barn, as he had promised, and the pony was worse. His eyes were almost closed now, and his breath whistled shrilly past an obstruction in his nose. A film covered that part of the eyes that was visible at all. It was doubtful whether the pony could see any more. Now and then he snorted, to clear his nose, and by the action seemed to plug it tighter. Jody looked dispiritedly at the pony's coat. The hair lay rough and unkempt and seemed to have lost all of its old lustre. Billy stood quietly beside the stall. Jody hated to ask, but he had to know.

'Billy, is he – is he going to get well?'

Billy put his fingers between the bars under the pony's jaw and felt about. 'Feel there,' he said and he guided Jody's fingers to a large lump under the jaw. 'When that gets bigger, I'll open it up and then he'll get better.'

Jody looked quickly away, for he had heard about that lump. 'What is it the matter with him?'

Billy didn't want to answer, but he had to. He

couldn't be wrong three times. 'Strangles,' he said shortly, 'but don't you worry about that. I'll pull him out of it. I've seen them get well when they were worse than Gabilan is. I'm going to steam him now. You can help.'

'Yes,' Jody said miserably. He followed Billy into the grain-room and watched him make the steaming bag ready. It was a long canvas nose-bag with straps to go over a horse's ears. Billy filled it one-third full of bran and then he added a couple of handfuls of dried hops. On top of the dry substance he poured a little carbolic acid and a little turpentine. 'I'll be mixing it all up while you run to the house for a kettle of boiling water,' Billy said.

When Jody came back with the steaming kettle, Billy buckled the straps over Gabilan's head and fitted the bag tightly around his nose. Then through a little hole in the side of the bag he poured the boiling water on the mixture. The pony started away as a cloud of strong steam rose up, but then the soothing fumes crept through his nose and into his lungs, and the sharp steam began to clear out the nasal passages. He breathed loudly. His legs trembled in an ague, and his eyes closed against the biting cloud. Billy poured in more water and kept the steam rising for fifteen minutes. At last he set down the kettle and took the bag from Gabilan's nose. The pony looked better. He breathed freely, and his eyes were open wider than they had been.

'See how good it makes him feel,' Billy said. 'Now

we'll wrap him up in the blanket again. Maybe he'll be nearly well by morning.'

'I'll stay with him to-night,' Jody suggested.

'No. Don't you do it. I'll bring my blankets down here and put them in the hay. You can stay to-morrow and steam him if he needs it.'

The evening was falling when they went to the house for their supper. Jody didn't even realise that someone else had fed the chickens and filled the wood-box. He walked up past the house to the dark brush line and took a drink of water from the tub. The spring water was so cold that it stung his mouth and drove a shiver through him. The sky above the hills was still light. He saw a hawk flying so high that it caught the sun on its breast and shone like a spark. Two blackbirds were driving him down the sky, glittering as they attacked their enemy. In the west the clouds were moving in to rain again.

Jody's father didn't speak at all while the family ate supper, but after Billy Buck had taken his blankets and gone to sleep in the barn, Carl Tiflin built a high fire in the fireplace and told stories. He told about the wild man who ran naked through the country and had a tail and ears like a horse, and he told about the rabbit-cats of Moro Cojo that hopped into the trees for birds. He revived the famous Maxwell brothers who found a vein of gold and hid the traces of it so carefully that they could never find it again.

Jody sat with his chin in his hands; his mouth worked nervously, and his father gradually became aware that

he wasn't listening very carefully. 'Isn't that funny?' he
asked.

Jody laughed politely and said, 'Yes, sir.' His father
was angry and hurt then. He didn't tell any more stories.
After a while, Jody took a lantern and went down to the
barn. Billy Buck was asleep in the hay, and, except that
his breath rasped a little in his lungs, the pony seemed
to be much better. Jody stayed a little while, running his
fingers over the rough red coat, and then he took up the
lantern and went back to the house. When he was in
bed, his mother came into the room.

'Have you enough covers on? It's getting winter.'

'Yes, ma'am.'

'Well, get some rest to-night.' She hesitated to go out,
stood uncertainly. 'The pony will be all right,' she said.

Jody was tired. He went to sleep quickly and didn't
awaken until dawn. The triangle sounded, and Billy
Buck came up from the barn before Jody could get out
of the house.

'How is he?' Jody demanded.

Billy always wolfed his breakfast. 'Pretty good. I'm
going to open that lump this morning. Then he'll be
better maybe.'

After breakfast Billy got out his best knife, one with a
needle point. He whetted the shining blade a long time
on a little carborundum stone. He tried the point and the
blade again and again on his calloused thumb-ball, and
at last he tried it on his upper lip.

On the way to the barn, Jody noticed how the young grass was up and how the stubble was melting day by day into the new green crop of volunteer. It was a cold sunny morning.

As soon as he saw the pony, Jody knew he was worse. His eyes were closed and sealed shut with dried mucus. His head hung so low that his nose almost touched the straw of his bed. There was a little groan in each breath, a deep-seated, patient groan.

Billy lifted the weak head and made a quick slash with the knife. Jody saw the yellow pus run out. He held up the head while Billy swabbed out the wound with weak carbolic acid salve.

'Now he'll feel better,' Billy assured him. 'That yellow poison is what makes him sick.'

Jody looked unbelieving at Billy Buck. 'He's awful sick.'

Billy thought a long time what to say. He nearly tossed off a careless assurance, but he saved himself in time. 'Yes, he's pretty sick,' he said at last. 'I've seen worse ones get well. If he doesn't get pneumonia, we'll pull him through. You stay with him. If he gets worse, you can come and get me.'

For a long time after Billy went away Jody stood beside the pony, stroking him behind the ears. The pony didn't flip his head the way he had done when he was well. The groaning in his breathing was becoming more hollow.

Doubletree Mutt looked into the barn, his big tail

waving provocatively, and Jody was so incensed at his health that he found a hard black clod on the floor and deliberately threw it. Doubletree Mutt went yelping away to nurse a bruised paw.

In the middle of the morning Billy Buck came back and made another steam-bag. Jody watched to see whether the pony improved this time as he had before. His breathing eased a little, but he did not raise his head.

The Saturday dragged on. Late in the afternoon Jody went to the house and brought his bedding down and made up a place to sleep in the hay. He didn't ask permission. He knew from the way his mother looked at him that she would let him do almost anything. That night he left a lantern burning on a wire over the box stall. Billy had told him to rub the pony's legs every little while.

At nine o'clock the wind sprang up and howled around the barn. And in spite of his worry, Jody grew sleepy. He got into his blankets and went to sleep, but the breathy groans of the pony sounded in his dreams. And in his sleep he heard a crashing noise which went on and on until it awakened him. The wind was rushing through the barn. He sprang up and looked down the lane of the stalls. The barn door had blown open, and the pony was gone.

He caught the lantern and ran outside into the gale, and he saw Gabilan weakly shambling away into the darkness, head down, legs working slowly and mechanically. When Jody ran up and caught him by the forelock, he allowed himself to be led back and put into his stall. His groans were louder, and a fierce whistling came from his nose. Jody didn't sleep any more then. The hissing of the pony's breath grew louder and sharper.

He was glad when Billy Buck came in at dawn. Billy looked for a time at the pony as though he had never seen him before. He felt the ears and flanks. 'Jody,' he said, 'I've got to do something you won't want to see. You run up to the house for a while.'

Jody grabbed him fiercely by the forearm. 'You're not going to shoot him?'

Billy patted his hand. 'No. I'm going to open a little hole in his windpipe so he can breathe. His nose is filled up. When he gets well, we'll put a little brass button in the hole for him to breathe through.'

Jody couldn't have gone away if he had wanted to. It was awful to see the red hide cut, but infinitely more terrible to know it was being cut and not to see it. 'I'll stay right here,' he said bitterly. 'You sure you got to?'

'Yes. I'm sure. If you stay, you can hold his head. If it doesn't make you sick, that is.'

The fine knife came out again and was whetted again just as carefully as it had been the first time. Jody held the pony's head up and the throat taut, while Billy felt up and down for the right place. Jody sobbed once as the bright knife-point disappeared into the throat. The pony plunged weakly away and then stood still, trembling violently. The blood ran thickly out and up the knife and across Billy's hand and into his shirt-sleeve. The sure square hand sawed out a round hole in the flesh, and the breath came bursting out of the hole, throwing a fine spray of blood. With the rush of oxygen, the pony took a sudden strength. He lashed out with his hind feet and tried to rear, but Jody held his head down while Billy mopped the new wound with carbolic salve. It was a good job. The blood stopped flowing and the air puffed out the hole and sucked it in regularly with a little bubbling noise.

The rain brought in by the night wind began to fall on the barn roof. Then the triangle rang for breakfast. 'You go up and eat while I wait,' Billy said. 'We've got to keep this hole from plugging up.'

Jody walked slowly out of the barn. He was too dispirited to tell Billy the barn door had blown open and let the pony out. He emerged into the wet grey morning and sloshed up to the house, taking a perverse pleasure in splashing through all the puddles. His mother fed him and put dry clothes on. She didn't question him. She seemed to know he couldn't answer questions. But when he was ready to go back to the barn she brought him a pan of steaming meal. 'Give him this,' she said.

But Jody did not take the pan. He said, 'He won't eat anything,' and ran out of the house. At the barn, Billy showed him how to fix a ball of cotton on a stick, with which to swab out the breathing-hole when it became clogged with mucus.

Jody's father walked into the barn and stood with

them in front of the stall. At length he turned to the boy. 'Hadn't you better come with me? I'm going to drive over the hill.' Jody shook his head. 'You better come on, out of this,' his father insisted.

Billy turned on him angrily. 'Let him alone. It's his pony, isn't it?'

Carl Tiflin walked away without saying another word. His feelings were badly hurt.

All morning Jody kept the wound open and the air passing in and out freely. At noon the pony lay wearily down on his side and stretched his nose out.

Billy came back. 'If you're going to stay with him to-night, you had better take a little nap,' he said. Jody went absently out of the barn. The sky had cleared to a hard thin blue. Everywhere the birds were busy with worms that had come to the damp surface of the ground.

Jody walked to the brush line and sat on the edge of the mossy tub. He looked down at the house and at the old bunk-house and at the dark cypress tree. The place was familiar, but curiously changed. It wasn't itself any more, but a frame for things that were happening. A cold wind blew out of the east now, signifying that the rain was over for a little while. At his feet Jody could see the little arms of new weeds spreading out over the ground. In the mud about the spring were thousands of quail tracks.

Doubletree Mutt came sideways and embarrassed up through the vegetable patch, and Jody, remembering how he had thrown the clod, put his arm about the dog's neck and kissed him on his wide black nose. Doubletree Mutt sat still, as though he knew some solemn thing was happening. His big tail slapped the ground gravely. Jody pulled a swollen tick out of Mutt's neck and popped it dead between his thumb-nails. It was a nasty thing. He washed his hands in the cold spring water.

Except for the steady swish of the wind, the farm was very quiet. Jody knew his mother wouldn't mind if he didn't go in to eat his lunch. After a little while he went slowly back to the barn. Mutt crept into his own little house and whined softly to himself for a long time.

Billy Buck stood up from the box and surrendered the cotton swab. The pony still lay on his side and the wound in his throat bellowed in and out. When Jody saw how dry and dead the hair looked, he knew at last that there was no hope for the pony. He had seen the dead hair before on dogs and on cows, and it was a sure sign. He sat heavily on the box and let down the barrier of the box stall. For a long time he kept his eyes on the moving wound, and at last he dozed, and the afternoon passed quickly. Just before dark his mother brought a deep dish of stew and left it for him and went away. Jody ate a little of it, and when it was dark he set the lantern on the floor by the pony's head so he could watch the wound and keep it open. And he dozed again until the night chill awakened him. The wind was blowing fiercely, bringing the north cold with it. Jody brought a blanket from his bed in the hay and wrapped himself in it.

Gabilan's breathing was quiet at last; the hole in his throat moved gently. The owls flew through the hayloft, shrieking and looking for mice. Jody put his hands down on his head and slept. In his sleep he was aware that the wind had increased. He heard it slamming about the barn.

It was daylight when he awakened. The barn door had swung open. The pony was gone. He sprang up and ran out into the morning light.

The pony's tracks were plain enough, dragging through the frost-like dew on the young grass, tired tracks with little lines between them where the hoofs had dragged. They headed for the brush line halfway up the ridge. Jody broke into a run and followed them. The sun shone on the sharp white quartz that stuck through the ground here and there. As he followed the plain trail, a shadow cut across in front of him. He looked up and saw a high circle of black buzzards, and the slowly revolving circle dropped lower and lower. The solemn birds soon disappeared over the ridge. Jody ran faster then, forced on by panic and rage. The trail entered the brush at last and followed a winding route among the tall sage bushes.

At the top of the ridge Jody was winded. He paused, puffing noisily. The blood pounded in his ears. Then he saw what he was looking for. Below, in one of the little clearings in the brush, lay the red pony. In the distance, Jody could see the legs moving slowly and convulsively. And in a circle around him stood the buzzards, waiting for the moment of death they know so well.

Jody leaped forward and plunged down the hill. The wet ground muffled his steps and the brush hid him. When he arrived, it was all over. The first buzzard sat on the pony's head. Jody plunged into the circle like a cat. The black brotherhood arose in a cloud, but the big one on the pony's head was too late. As it hopped along to take off, Jody caught its wing tip and pulled it down. It was nearly as big as he was. The free wing crashed into his face with the force of a club, but he hung on. The claws fastened on his leg and the wing elbows battered his head on either side. Jody groped blindly with his free hand. His fingers found the neck of the struggling bird. The red eyes looked into his face, calm and fearless and fierce; the naked head turned from side to side. Jody brought up his knee and fell on the great bird. He held the neck to the ground with one hand while his other found a piece of sharp white quartz. The red fearless eyes still looked at him, impersonal and un-afraid and detached. He struck again and again, until the buzzard lay dead. He was still beating the dead bird when Billy Buck pulled him off and held him tightly to calm his shaking.

Carl Tiflin wiped the blood from the boy's face with a red bandana. Jody was limp and quiet now. His father moved the buzzard with his toe. 'Jody,' he explained, 'the buzzard didn't kill the pony. Don't you know that?'

'I know it,' Jody said wearily.

It was Billy Buck who was angry. He had lifted Jody in his arms, and had turned to carry him home. But he turned back on Carl Tiflin. ' 'Course he knows it,' Billy said furiously. 'Good God! man, can't you see how he'd feel about it?'

2

The Great Mountains

IN THE HUMMING HEAT OF A MIDSUMMER AFTER-noon the little boy Jody listlessly looked about the ranch for something to do. He had been to the barn, had thrown rocks at the swallows' nests under the eaves until every one of the little mud houses broke open and dropped its lining of straw and dirty feathers. Then at the ranch-house he baited a rat-trap with stale cheese and set it where Doubletree Mutt, that good big dog, would get his nose snapped. Jody was not moved by an impulse of cruelty; he was bored with the long hot afternoon. Doubletree Mutt put his stupid nose in the trap and got it smacked, and shrieked with agony and limped away with blood on his nostrils. No matter where he was hurt, Mutt limped. It was just a way he had. Once when he was young, Mutt got caught in a coyote trap, and always after that he limped, even when he was scolded.

When Mutt yelped, Jody's mother called from inside the house, 'Jody! Stop torturing that dog and find something to do.'

Jody felt mean then, so he threw a rock at Mutt. Then he took his slingshot from the porch and walked up toward the brush line to try to kill a bird. It was a good slingshot, with store-bought rubbers, but while Jody had often shot at birds, he had never hit one. He walked up through the vegetable patch, kicking his bare toes into the dust. And on the way he found the perfect slingshot stone, round and slightly flattened and heavy enough to carry through the air. He fitted it into the leather pouch of his weapon and proceeded to the brush line. His eyes narrowed, his mouth worked strenuously; for the first time that afternoon he was intent. In the shade of the sagebrush the little birds were working, scratching in the leaves, flying restlessly a few feet and scratching again. Jody pulled back the rubbers of the sling and advanced cautiously. One little thrush paused and looked at him and crouched, ready to fly. Jody sidled nearer, moving one foot slowly after the other. When he was twenty feet away, he carefully raised the sling and aimed. The stone whizzed; the thrush started up and flew right into it. And down the little bird went with a broken head. Jody ran to it and picked it up.

'Well, I got you,' he said.

The bird looked much smaller dead than it had alive. Jody felt a little mean pain in his stomach, so he took out his pocket-knife and cut off the bird's head. Then he disembowelled it, and took off its wings; and finally he threw all the pieces into the brush. He didn't care about the bird, or its life, but he knew what older people would say if they had seen him kill it; he was ashamed because of their potential opinion. He decided to forget the whole thing as quickly as he could, and never to mention it.

The hills were dry at this season, and the wild grass was golden, but where the spring-pipe filled the round tub and the tub spilled over, there lay a stretch of fine green grass, deep and sweet and moist. Jody drank from the mossy tub and washed the bird's blood from his hands in cold water. Then he lay on his back in the grass and looked up at the dumpling summer clouds. By closing one eye and destroying perspective he brought them down within reach so that he could put up his fingers and stroke them. He helped the gentle wind push them down the sky; it seemed to him that they went faster for his help. One fat white cloud he helped clear to the mountain rims and pressed it firmly over, out of sight. Jody wondered what it was seeing then. He sat up the better to look at the great mountains where they went piling back, growing darker and more savage until they finished with one jagged ridge, high up against the west. Curious secret mountains; he thought of the little he knew about them.

'What's on the other side?' he asked his father once.

'More mountains, I guess. Why?'

'And on the other side of them?'

'More mountains. Why?'

'More mountains on and on?'

'Well, no. At last you come to the ocean.'

'But what's in the mountains?'

'Just cliffs and brush and rocks and dryness.'

'Were you ever there?'

'No.'

'Has anybody ever been there?'

'A few people, I guess. It's dangerous, with cliffs and things. Why, I've read there's more unexplored country in the mountains of Monterey County than any place in the United States.' His father seemed proud that this should be so.

'And at last the ocean?'

'At last the ocean.'

'But,' the boy insisted, 'but in between? No one knows?'

'Oh, a few people do, I guess. But there's nothing there to get. And not much water. Just rocks and cliffs and greasewood. Why?'

'It would be good to go.'

'What for? There's nothing there.'

Jody knew something was there, something very wonderful because it wasn't known, something secret and mysterious. He could feel within himself that this was so. He said to his mother, 'Do you know what's in the big mountains?'

She looked at him and then back at the ferocious range, and she said, 'Only the bear, I guess.'

'What bear?'

'Why, the one that went over the mountain to see what he could see.'

Jody questioned Billy Buck, the ranch hand, about the possibility of ancient cities lost in the mountains, but Billy agreed with Jody's father.

'It ain't likely,' Billy said. 'There'd be nothing to eat unless a kind of people that can eat rocks live there.'

That was all the information Jody ever got, and it made the mountains dear to him, and terrible. He thought often of the miles of ridge after ridge until at last there was the sea. When the peaks were pink in the morning they invited him among them; and when the sun had gone over the edge in the evening and the mountains were a purple-like despair, then Jody was afraid of them; then they were so impersonal and aloof that their very imperturbability was a threat.

Now he turned his head toward the mountains of the east, the Gabilans, and they were jolly mountains, with hill ranches in their creases, and with pine trees growing on the crests. People lived there, and battles had been fought against the Mexicans on the slopes. He looked back for an instant at the Great Ones and shivered a little at the contrast. The foot-hill cup of the home ranch below him was sunny and safe. The house gleamed with white light and the barn was brown and warm. The red cows on the farther hill ate their way slowly toward the north. Even the dark cypress tree by the bunk-house was usual and safe. The chickens scratched about in the dust of the farmyard with quick waltzing steps.

Then a moving figure caught Jody's eye. A man walked slowly over the brow of the hill, on the road from Salinas, and he was headed toward the house. Jody stood up and moved down toward the house too, for if someone was coming he wanted to be there to see. By the time the boy had got to the house the walking man was only halfway down the road, a lean man, very straight in the shoulders. Jody could tell he was old only because his heels struck the ground with hard jerks. As he approached nearer, Jody saw that he was dressed in blue jeans and in a coat of the same material. He wore clod-hopper shoes and an old flat-brimmed Stetson hat. Over his shoulder he carried a gunny sack, lumpy and full. In a few moments he had trudged close enough so that his face could be seen. And his face was as dark as dried beef. A moustache, blue-white against the dark skin, hovered over his mouth, and his hair was white too, where it showed at his neck. The skin of his face had shrunk back against the skull until it defined bone, not flesh, and made the nose and chin seem sharp and fragile. The eyes were large and deep and dark, with eyelids stretched tightly over them. Irises and pupils were one, and very black, but the eyeballs were brown. There were no wrinkles in the face at all. This old man wore a blue denim coat buttoned to the throat with brass buttons, as all men do who wear no shirts. Out of the sleeves came strong bony wrists and hands gnarled and knotted and hard as peach branches. The nails were flat and blunt and shiny.

The old man drew close to the gate and swung down his sack when he confronted Jody. His lips fluttered a little and a soft impersonal voice came from between them.

'Do you live here?'

Jody was embarrassed. He turned and looked at the house, and he turned back and looked toward the barn where his father and Billy Buck were. 'Yes,' he said, when no help came from either direction.

'I have come back,' the old man said. 'I am Gitano, and I have come back.'

Jody could not take all this responsibility. He turned abruptly, and ran into the house for help, and the screen door banged after him. His mother was in the kitchen poking out the clogged holes on a colander with a hairpin, and biting her lower lip with concentration.

'It's an old man,' Jody cried excitedly. 'It's an old paisano[1] man, and he says he's come back.'

His mother put down the colander and stuck the hairpin behind the sink board. 'What's the matter now?' she asked patiently.

1. Peasant.

'It's an old man outside. Come on out.'

'Well, what does he want?' She untied the strings of her apron and smoothed her hair with her fingers.

'I don't know. He came walking.'

His mother smoothed down her dress and went out, and Jody followed her. Gitano had not moved.

'Yes?' Mrs Tiflin asked.

Gitano took off his old black hat and held it with both hands in front of him. He repeated, 'I am Gitano, and I have come back.'

'Come back? Back where?'

Gitano's whole straight body leaned forward a little. His right hand described the circle of the hills, the sloping fields and the mountains, and ended at his hat again. 'Back to the rancho. I was born here, and my father, too.'

'Here?' she demanded. 'This isn't an old place.'

'No, there,' he said, pointing to the western ridge. 'On the other side there, in a house that is gone.'

At last she understood. 'The old 'dobe that's washed almost away, you mean?'

'Yes, señora. When the rancho broke up they put no more lime on the 'dobe, and the rains washed it down.'

Jody's mother was silent for a little, and curious home-sick thoughts ran through her mind, but quickly she cleared them out. 'And what do you want here now, Gitano?'

'I will stay here,' he said quietly, 'until I die.'

'But we don't need an extra man here.'

'I cannot work hard any more, señora. I can milk a

cow, feed chickens, cut a little wood, no more. I will stay here.' He indicated the sack on the ground beside him. 'Here are my things.'

She turned to Jody. 'Run down to the barn and call your father.'

Jody dashed away, and he returned with Carl Tiflin and Billy Buck behind him. The old man was standing as he had been, but he was resting now. His whole body had sagged into a timeless repose.

'What is it?' Carl Tiflin asked. 'What's Jody so excited about?'

Mrs Tiflin motioned to the old man. 'He wants to stay here. He wants to do a little work and stay here.'

'Well, we can't have him. We don't need any more men. He's too old. Billy does everything we need.'

They had been talking over him as though he did not exist, and now, suddenly, they both hesitated and looked at Gitano and were embarrassed.

He cleared his throat. 'I am too old to work. I come back where I was born.'

'You weren't born here,' Carl said sharply.

'No. In the 'dobe house over the hill. It was all one rancho before you came.'

'In the mud house that's all melted down?'

'Yes. I and my father. I will stay here now on the rancho.'

'I tell you you won't stay,' Carl said angrily. 'I don't need an old man. This isn't a big ranch. I can't afford food and doctor bills for an old man. You must have relatives and friends. Go to them. It is like begging to come to strangers.'

'I was born here,' Gitano said patiently and inflexibly.

Carl Tiflin didn't like to be cruel, but he felt he must. 'You can eat here to-night,' he said. 'You can sleep in the little room of the old bunk-house. We'll give you your breakfast in the morning, and then you'll have to go along. Go to your friends. Don't come to die with strangers.'

Gitano put on his black hat and stooped for the sack. 'Here are my things,' he said.

Carl turned away. 'Come on, Billy, we'll finish down at the barn. Jody, show him the little room in the bunk-house.'

He and Billy turned back toward the barn. Mrs Tiflin went into the house, saying over her shoulder, 'I'll send some blankets down.'

Gitano looked questioningly at Jody. 'I'll show you where it is,' Jody said.

There was a cot with a shuck mattress, an apple-box holding a tin lantern, and a backless rocking-chair in the little room of the bunk-house. Gitano laid his sack carefully on the floor and sat down on the bed. Jody stood shyly in the room, hesitating to go. At last he said:

'Did you come out of the big mountains?'

Gitano shook his head slowly. 'No, I worked down the Salinas Valley.'

The afternoon thought would not let Jody go. 'Did you ever go into the big mountains back there?'

The old dark eyes grew fixed, and their light turned inward on the years that were living in Gitano's head. 'Once – when I was a little boy. I went with my father.'

'Way back, clear into the mountains?'

'Yes.'

'What was there?' Jody cried. 'Did you see any people or any houses?'

'No.'

'Well, what was there?'

Gitano's eyes remained inward. A little wrinkled strain came between his brows.

'What did you see in there?' Jody repeated.

'I don't know,' Gitano said. 'I don't remember.'

'Was it terrible and dry?'

'I don't remember.'

In his excitement, Jody had lost his shyness. 'Don't you remember anything about it?'

Gitano's mouth opened for a word, and remained open while his brain sought the word. 'I think it was quiet – I think it was nice.'

Gitano's eyes seemed to have found something back in the years, for they grew soft and a little smile seemed to come and go in them.

'Didn't you ever go back in the mountains again?' Jody insisted.

'No.'

'Didn't you ever want to?'

But now Gitano's face became impatient. 'No,' he said

in a tone that told Jody he didn't want to talk about it any more. The boy was held by a curious fascination. He didn't want to go away from Gitano. His shyness returned.

'Would you like to come down to the barn and see the stock?' he asked.

Gitano stood up and put on his hat and prepared to follow.

It was almost evening now. They stood near the watering trough while the horses sauntered in from the hillsides for an evening drink. Gitano rested his big twisted hands on the top rail of the fence. Five horses came down and drank, and then stood about, nibbling at the dirt or rubbing their sides against the polished wood of the fence. Long after they had finished drinking, an old horse appeared over the brow of the hill and came painfully down. It had long yellow teeth; its hooves were flat and sharp as spades, and its ribs and hip-bones jutted out under its skin. It hobbled up to the trough and drank water with a loud sucking noise.

'That's old Easter,' Jody explained. 'That's the first horse my father ever had. He's thirty years old.' He looked up into Gitano's old eyes for some response.

'No good any more,' Gitano said.

Jody's father and Billy Buck came out of the barn and walked over.

'Too old to work,' Gitano repeated. 'Just eats and pretty soon dies.'

Carl Tiflin caught the last words. He hated his

brutality toward old Gitano, and so he became brutal again.

'It's a shame not to shoot old Easter,' he said. 'It'd save him a lot of pains and rheumatism.' He looked secretly at Gitano, to see whether he noticed the parallel, but the big bony hands did not move, nor did the dark eyes turn from the horse. 'Old things ought to be put out of their misery,' Jody's father went on. 'One shot, a big noise, one big pain in the head maybe, and that's all. That's better than stiffness and sore teeth.'

Billy Buck broke in. 'They got a right to rest after they worked all of their life. Maybe they like to just walk around.'

Carl had been looking steadily at the skinny horse. 'You can't imagine now what Easter used to look like,' he said softly. 'High neck, deep chest, fine barrel. He could jump a five-bar gate in stride. I won a flat race on him when I was fifteen years old. I could of got two hundred dollars for him any time. You wouldn't think how pretty he was.' He checked himself, for he hated softness. 'But he ought to be shot now,' he said.

'He's got a right to rest,' Billy Buck insisted.

Jody's father had a humorous thought. He turned to Gitano. 'If ham and eggs grew on a side-hill I'd turn you out to pasture too,' he said. 'But I can't afford to pasture you in my kitchen.'

He laughed to Billy Buck about it as they went on toward the house. 'Be a good thing for all of us if ham and eggs grew on the side-hills.'

Jody knew how his father was probing for a place to hurt in Gitano. He had been probed often. His father knew every place in the boy where a word would fester.

'He's only talking,' Jody said. 'He didn't mean it about shooting Easter. He likes Easter. That was the first horse he ever owned.'

The sun sank behind the high mountains as they stood there, and the ranch was hushed. Gitano seemed to be more at home in the evening. He made a curious sharp sound with his lips and stretched one of his hands over the fence. Old Easter moved stiffly to him, and Gitano rubbed the lean neck under the mane.

'You like him?' Jody asked softly.

'Yes – but he's no damn good.'

The triangle sounded at the ranch-house. 'That's supper,' Jody cried. 'Come on up to supper.'

As they walked up toward the house Jody noticed again that Gitano's body was as straight as that of a young man. Only by a jerkiness in his movements and by the scuffling of his heels could it be seen that he was old.

The turkeys were flying heavily into the lower branches of the cypress tree by the bunk-house. A fat sleek ranch cat walked across the road carrying a rat so large that its tail dragged on the ground. The quail on the side-hills were still sounding the clear water call.

Jody and Gitano came to the back steps and Mrs Tiflin looked out through the screen door at them.

'Come running, Jody. Come in to supper, Gitano.'

Carl and Billy Buck had started to eat at the long oil-cloth-covered table. Jody slipped into his chair without moving it, but Gitano stood holding his hat until Carl looked up and said, 'Sit down, sit down. You might as well get your belly full before you go on.' Carl was afraid he might relent and let the old man stay, and so he continued to remind himself that this couldn't be.

Gitano laid his hat on the floor and diffidently sat down. He wouldn't reach for food. Carl had to pass it to him. 'Here, fill yourself up.' Gitano ate very slowly, cutting tiny pieces of meat and arranging little pats of mashed potato on his plate.

The situation would not stop worrying Carl Tiflin. 'Haven't you got any relatives in this part of the country?' he asked.

Gitano answered with some pride, 'My brother-in-law's in Monterey. I have cousins there, too.'

'Well, you can go and live there, then.'

'I was born here,' Gitano said in gentle rebuke.

Jody's mother came in from the kitchen, carrying a large bowl of tapioca pudding.

Carl chuckled to her, 'Did I tell you what I said to him? I said if ham and eggs grew on the side-hills I'd put him out to pasture, like old Easter.'

Gitano stared unmoved at his plate.

'It's too bad he can't stay,' said Mrs Tiflin.

'Now don't start anything,' Carl said crossly.

When they had finished eating, Carl and Billy Buck and Jody went into the living-room to sit for a while, but

Gitano, without a word of farewell or thanks, walked through the kitchen and out the back door. Jody sat and secretly watched his father. He knew how mean his father felt.

'This country's full of these old paisanos,' Carl said to Billy Buck.

'They're damn good men,' Billy defended them. 'They can work older than white men. I saw one of them a hundred and five years old, and he could still ride a horse. You don't see any white men as old as Gitano walking twenty or thirty miles.'

'Oh, they're tough, all right,' Carl agreed. 'Say, are you standing up for him, too? Listen, Billy,' he explained, 'I'm having a hard enough time keeping this ranch out of the Bank of Italy without taking on anybody else to feed. You know that, Billy.'

'Sure, I know,' said Billy. 'If you was rich, it'd be different.'

'That's right, and it isn't like he didn't have relatives to go to. A brother-in-law and cousins right in Monterey. Why should I worry about him?'

Jody sat quietly listening, and he seemed to hear Gitano's gentle voice and its unanswerable, 'But I was born here.' Gitano was mysterious like the mountains. There were ranges back as far as you could see, but behind the last range piled up against the sky there was a great unknown country. And Gitano was an old man, until you got to the dull dark eyes. And in behind them was some unknown thing. He didn't ever say enough to let you guess what was inside, under the eyes. Jody felt himself irresistibly drawn toward the bunk-house. He slipped from his chair while his father was talking and he went out the door without making a sound.

The night was very dark and far-off noises carried in clearly. The hamebells of a wood team sounded from way over the hill on the county road. Jody picked his way across the dark yard. He could see a light through the window of the little room of the bunk-house. Because the night was secret he walked quietly up to the window and peered in. Gitano sat in the rocking-chair and his back was toward the window. His right arm moved slowly back and forth in front of him. Jody pushed the door open and walked in. Gitano jerked upright and, seizing a piece of deerskin, he tried to throw it over the thing in his lap, but the skin slipped away. Jody stood overwhelmed by the thing in Gitano's hand, a lean and lovely rapier with a golden basket hilt. The blade was like a thin ray of dark light. The hilt was pierced and intricately carved.

'What is it?' Jody demanded.

Gitano only looked at him with resentful eyes, and he picked up the fallen deerskin and firmly wrapped the beautiful blade in it.

Jody put out his hand. 'Can't I see it?'

Gitano's eyes smouldered angrily and he shook his head.

'Where'd you get it? Where'd it come from?'

Now Gitano regarded him profoundly, as though he

pondered. 'I got it from my father.'

'Well, where'd he get it?'

Gitano looked down at the long deerskin parcel in his hand. 'I don' know.'

'Didn't he ever tell you?'

'No.'

'What do you do with it?'

Gitano looked slightly surprised. 'Nothing. I just keep it.'

'Can't I see it again?'

The old man slowly unwrapped the shining blade and let the lamplight slip along it for a moment. Then he wrapped it up again. 'You go now. I want to go to bed.' He blew out the lamp almost before Jody had closed the door.

As he went back towards the house, Jody knew one thing more sharply than he had ever known anything. He must never tell anyone about the rapier. It would be a dreadful thing to tell anyone about it, for it would destroy some fragile structure of truth. It was a truth that might be shattered by division.

On the way across the dark yard Jody passed Billy Buck. 'They're wondering where you are,' Billy said.

Jody slipped into the living-room, and his father turned to him. 'Where have you been?'

'I just went out to see if I caught any rats in my new trap.'

'It's time you went to bed,' his father said.

    ·   ·   ·   ·   ·

Jody was first at the breakfast table in the morning. Then his father came in, and last, Billy Buck. Mrs Tiflin looked in from the kitchen.

'Where's the old man, Billy?' she asked.

'I guess he's out walking,' Billy said. 'I looked in his room and he wasn't there.'

'Maybe he started early to Monterey,' said Carl. 'It's a long walk.'

'No,' Billy explained. 'His sack is in the little room.'

After breakfast Jody walked down to the bunk-house. Flies were flashing about in the sunshine. The ranch seemed especially quiet this morning. When he was sure no one was watching him, Jody went into the little room, and looked into Gitano's sack. An extra pair of long cotton underwear was there, an extra pair of jeans and three pairs of worn socks. Nothing else was in the sack. A sharp loneliness fell on Jody. He walked slowly back toward the house. His father stood on the porch talking to Mrs Tiflin.

'I guess old Easter's dead at last,' he said. 'I didn't see him come down to water with the other horses.'

In the middle of the morning Jess Taylor from the ridge ranch rode down.

'You didn't sell that old grey crowbait of yours, did you, Carl?'

'No, of course not. Why?'

'Well,' Jess said, 'I was out this morning early, and I saw a funny thing. I saw an old man on an old horse, no saddle, only a piece of rope for a bridle. He wasn't on the road at all. He was cutting right up straight through the brush. I think he had a gun. At least I saw something shine in his hand.'

'That's old Gitano,' Carl Tiflin said. 'I'll see if any of my guns are missing.' He stepped into the house for a second. 'Nope, all here. Which way was he heading, Jess?'

'Well, that's the funny thing. He was heading straight back into the mountains.'

Carl laughed. 'They never get too old to steal,' he said. 'I guess he just stole old Easter.'

'Want to go after him, Carl?'

'Hell no, just save me burying that horse. I wonder where he got the gun. I wonder what he wants back there.'

Jody walked up through the vegetable patch, toward the brush line. He looked searchingly at the towering mountains – ridge after ridge after ridge until at last there was the ocean. For a moment he thought he could see a black speck crawling up the farthest ridge. Jody thought of the rapier and of Gitano. And he thought of the great mountains. A longing caressed him, and it was so sharp that he wanted to cry to get it out of his breast. He lay down in the green grass near the round tub at the brush line. He covered his eyes with his crossed arms and lay there a long time, and he was full of a nameless sorrow.

3
The Promise

IN A MID-AFTERNOON OF SPRING, THE LITTLE
boy Jody walked martially along the brush-lined
road toward his home ranch. Banging his knee against
the golden lard bucket he used for school lunch, he con-
trived a good bass drum, while his tongue fluttered
sharply against his teeth to fill in snare drums and
occasional trumpets. Some time back the other members
of the squad that walked so smartly from the school had

turned into the various little canyons and taken the wagon roads to their own home ranches. Now Jody marched seemingly alone, with high-lifted knees and pounding feet; but behind him there was a phantom army with great flags and swords, silent but deadly.

The afternoon was green and gold with spring. Underneath the spread branches of the oaks the plants grew pale and tall, and on the hills the feed was smooth and thick. The sagebrushes shone with new silver leaves and the oaks wore hoods of golden green. Over the hills there hung such a green odour that the horses on the flats galloped madly, and then stopped; wondering lambs, and even old sheep, jumped in the air unexpectedly and landed on stiff legs, and went on eating; young clumsy calves butted their heads together and drew back and butted again.

As the grey and silent army marched past, led by Jody, the animals stopped their feeding and their play and watched it go by.

Suddenly Jody stopped. The grey army halted, bewildered and nervous. Jody went down on his knees. The army stood in long uneasy ranks for a moment, and then, with a soft sigh of sorrow, rose up in a faint grey mist and disappeared. Jody had seen the thorny crown of a horny-toad moving under the dust of the road. His grimy hand went out and grasped the spiked halo and held firmly while the little beast struggled. Then Jody turned the horny-toad over, exposing its pale gold stomach. With a gentle forefinger he stroked the throat and chest until the horny-toad relaxed, until its eyes closed and it lay languorous and asleep.

Jody opened his lunch pail and deposited the first game inside. He moved on now, his knees bent slightly, his shoulders crouched; his bare feet were wise and silent. In his right hand there was a long grey rifle. The brush along the road stirred restively under a new and unexpected population of grey tigers and grey bears. The hunting was very good, for by the time Jody reached the fork of the road where the mail box stood on a post, he had captured two more horny-toads, four little grass lizards, a blue snake, sixteen yellow-winged grasshoppers and a brown damp newt from under a rock. This assortment scrabbled unhappily against the tin of the lunch bucket.

At the road fork the rifle evaporated and the tigers and bears melted from the hillsides. Even the moist and uncomfortable creatures in the lunch pail ceased to exist, for the little red metal flag was up on the mail box, signifying that some postal matter was inside. Jody set his pail on the ground and opened the letter box. There was a Montgomery Ward catalogue and a copy of the *Salinas Weekly Journal*. He slammed the box, picked up his lunch pail and trotted over the ridge and down into the cup of the ranch. Past the barn he ran, and past the used-up haystack and the bunk-house and the cypress tree. He banged through the front screen door of the ranch-house calling: 'Ma'am, ma'am, there's a catalogue.'

Mrs Tiflin was in the kitchen spooning clabbered milk into a cotton bag. She put down her work and rinsed her hands under the tap. 'Here in the kitchen, Jody. Here I am.'

He ran in and clattered his lunch pail on the sink. 'Here it is. Can I open the catalogue, ma'am?'

Mrs Tiflin took up the spoon again and went back to her cottage cheese. 'Don't lose it, Jody. Your father will want to see it.' She scraped the last of the milk into the bag. 'Oh, Jody, your father wants to see you before you go to your chores.' She waved a cruising fly from the cheese bag.

Jody closed the new catalogue in alarm. 'Ma'am?'

'Why don't you ever listen? I say your father wants to see you.'

The boy laid the catalogue gently on the sink board. 'Do you – it is something I did?'

Mrs Tiflin laughed. 'Always a bad conscience. What did you do?'

'Nothing, ma'am,' he said lamely. But he couldn't remember, and besides it was impossible to know what action might later be construed as a crime.

His mother hung the full bag on a nail where it could drip into the sink. 'He just said he wanted to see you when you got home. He's somewhere down by the barn.'

Jody turned and went out the back door. Hearing his mother open the lunch pail and then gasp with rage, a memory stabbed him and he trotted away toward the barn, conscientiously not hearing an angry voice that called him from the house.

Carl Tiflin and Billy Buck, the ranch hand, stood against the lower pasture fence. Each man rested one foot on the lowest bar and both elbows on the top bar. They were talking slowly and aimlessly. In the pasture half-a-dozen horses nibbled contentedly at the sweet grass. The mare, Nellie, stood backed up against the gate, rubbing her buttocks on the heavy post.

Jody sidled uneasily near. He dragged one foot to give an impression of great innocence and nonchalance. When he arrived beside the men he put one foot on the lowest fence-rail, rested his elbows on the second bar and looked into the pasture too. The two men glanced sideways at him.

'I wanted to see you,' Carl said in the stern tone he reserved for children and animals.

'Yes, sir,' said Jody guiltily.

'Billy, here, says you took good care of the pony before it died.'

No punishment was in the air. Jody grew bolder. 'Yes, sir, I did.'

'Billy says you have a good patient hand with horses.'

Jody felt a sudden warm friendliness for the ranch hand.

Billy put in, 'He trained that pony as good as anybody I ever seen.'

Then Carl Tiflin came gradually to the point. 'If you could have another horse would you work for it?'

Jody shivered. 'Yes, sir.'

'Well, look here, then. Billy says the best way for you to be a good hand with horses is to raise a colt.'

'It's the *only* good way,' Billy interrupted.

'Now, look here, Jody,' continued Carl. 'Jess Taylor, up to the ridge ranch, has a fair stallion, but it'll cost five dollars. I'll put up the money, but you'll have to work it out all summer. Will you do that?'

Jody felt his insides were shrivelling. 'Yes, sir,' he said softly.

'And no complaining? And no forgetting when you're told to do something?'

'Yes, sir.'

'Well, all right, then. To-morrow morning you take Nellie up to the ridge ranch and get her bred. You'll have to take care of her, too, till she throws the colt.'

'Yes, sir.'

'You better get to the chickens and the wood now.'

Jody slid away. In passing behind Billy Buck he very nearly put out his hands to touch the blue-jeaned legs. His shoulders swayed a little with maturity and importance.

He went to his work with unprecedented seriousness. This night he did not dump the can of grain to the chickens so that they had to leap over each other and struggle to get it. No, he spread the wheat so far and so carefully that the hens couldn't find some of it at all. And in the house, after listening to his mother's despair over boys who filled their lunch pails with slimy, suffocated reptiles, and bugs, he promised never to do it

again. Indeed, Jody felt that all such foolishness was lost in the past. He was far too grown up ever to put horny-toads in his lunch pail any more. He carried in so much wood and built such a high structure with it that his mother walked in fear of an avalanche of oak. When he was done, when he had gathered eggs that had remained hidden for weeks, Jody walked down again past the cypress tree, and past the bunk-house toward the pasture. A fat warty toad that looked out at him from under the watering trough had no emotional effect on him at all.

Carl Tiflin and Billy Buck were not in sight, but from a metallic ringing on the other side of the barn Jody knew that Billy Buck was just starting to milk a cow.

The other horses were eating towards the upper end of the pasture, but Nellie continued to rub herself nervously against the post. Jody walked slowly near, saying, 'So, girl, so-o, Nellie.' The mare's ears went back naughtily and her lips drew away from her yellow teeth. She turned her head around; her eyes were glazed and mad. Jody climbed to the top of the fence and hung his feet over and looked paternally down on the mare.

The evening hovered while he sat there. Bats and night-hawks flicked about. Billy Buck, walking toward the house carrying a full milk bucket, saw Jody and stopped. 'It's a long time to wait,' he said gently. 'You'll get awful tired waiting.'

'No, I won't, Billy. How long will it be?'

'Nearly a year.'

'Well, I won't get tired.'

The triangle at the house rang stridently. Jody climbed down from the fence and walked to supper beside Billy Buck. He even put out his hand and took hold of the milk bucket to help carry it.

The next morning after breakfast Carl Tiflin folded a five-dollar bill in a piece of newspaper and pinned the package in the bib pocket of Jody's overalls. Billy Buck haltered the mare, Nellie, and led her out of the pasture.

'Be careful now,' he warned. 'Hold her up short here so she can't bite you. She's crazy as a coot.'

Jody took hold of the halter leather itself and started up the hill toward the ridge ranch with Nellie skittering and jerking behind him. In the pasturage along the road the wild oat heads were just clearing their scabbards. The warm morning sun shone on Jody's back so sweetly that he was forced to take a serious stiff-legged hop now and then in spite of his maturity. On the fences the shiny blackbirds with red epaulettes clicked their dry call. The meadowlarks sang like water, and the wild doves, concealed among the bursting leaves of the oaks, made a sound of restrained grieving. In the fields the rabbits sat sunning themselves, with only their forked ears showing above the grass heads.

After an hour of steady uphill walking, Jody turned into a narrow road that led up a steeper hill to the ridge ranch. He could see the red roof of the barn sticking up above the oak trees, and he could hear a dog barking unemotionally near the house.

Suddenly Nellie jerked back and nearly freed herself.

From the direction of the barn Jody heard a shrill whistling scream and a splintering of wood, and then a man's voice shouting. Nellie reared and whinnied. When Jody held to the halter rope she ran at him with bared teeth. He dropped his hold and scutted out of the way, into the brush. The high scream came from the oaks again, and Nellie answered it. With hooves battering the ground the stallion appeared and charged down the

hill trailing a broken halter rope. His eyes glittered feverishly. His stiff, erected nostrils were as red as flame. His black, sleek hide shone in the sunlight. The stallion came on so fast that he couldn't stop when he reached the mare. Nellie's ears went back; she whirled and kicked at him as he went by. The stallion spun around and reared. He struck the mare with his front hoof, and while she staggered under the blow, his teeth raked her neck and drew an ooze of blood.

Instantly Nellie's mood changed. She became coquettishly feminine. She nibbled his arched neck with her lips. She edged around and rubbed her shoulder against his shoulder. Jody stood half-hidden in the brush and watched. He heard the step of a horse behind him, but before he could turn, a hand caught him by the overall straps and lifted him off the ground. Jess Taylor sat the boy behind him on the horse.

'You might have got killed,' he said. 'Sundog's a mean devil sometimes. He busted his rope and went right through a gate.'

Jody sat quietly, but in a moment he cried, 'He'll hurt her, he'll kill her. Get him away!'

Jess chuckled. 'She'll be all right. Maybe you'd better climb off and go up to the house for a little. You could get maybe a piece of pie up there.'

But Jody shook his head. 'She's mine, and the colt's going to be mine. I'm going to raise it up.'

Jess nodded. 'Yes, that's a good thing. Carl has good sense sometimes.'

In a little while the danger was over. Jess lifted Jody down and then caught the stallion by its broken halter rope. And he rode ahead, while Jody followed, leading Nellie.

It was only after he had unpinned and handed over the five dollars, and after he had eaten two pieces of pie, that Jody started for home again. And Nellie followed docilely after him. She was so quiet that Jody climbed on a stump and rode her most of the way home.

The five dollars his father had advanced reduced Jody to peonage for the whole late spring and summer. When the hay was cut he drove a rake. He led the horse that pulled on the Jackson-fork tackle, and when the baler came he drove the circling horse that put pressure on the bales. In addition, Carl Tiflin taught him to milk and put a cow under his care, so that a new chore was added night and morning.

The bay mare Nellie quickly grew complacent. As she walked about the yellowing hillsides or worked at easy tasks, her lips were curled in a perpetual fatuous smile. She moved slowly, with the calm importance of an empress. When she was put to a team, she pulled steadily and unemotionally. Jody went to see her every day. He studied her with critical eyes and saw no change whatever.

One afternoon Billy Buck leaned the many-tined manure fork against the barn wall. He loosened his belt and tucked in his shirt-tail and tightened the belt again. He picked one of the little straws from his hatband and put it in the corner of his mouth. Jody, who was helping Doubletree Mutt, the big serious dog, to dig out a gopher,[1] straightened up as the ranch hand sauntered out of the barn.

'Let's go up and have a look at Nellie,' Billy suggested.

Instantly Jody fell into step with him. Doubletree Mutt watched them over his shoulder; then he dug furiously, growled, sounded little sharp yelps to indicate that the gopher was practically caught. When he looked over his shoulder again, and saw that neither Jody nor Billy was interested, he climbed reluctantly out of the hole and followed them up the hill.

The wild oats were ripening. Every head bent sharply under its load of grain, and the grass was dry enough so that it made a swishing sound as Jody and Billy stepped through it. Halfway up the hill they could see Nellie and the iron-grey gelding, Pete, nibbling the heads from the wild oats. When they approached, Nellie looked at them and backed her ears and bobbed her head up and down rebelliously. Billy walked to her and put his hand under her mane and patted her neck, until her ears came forward again and she nibbled delicately at his shirt.

Jody asked, 'Do you think she's really going to have a colt?'

Billy rolled the lids back from the mare's eyes with his thumb and forefinger. He felt the lower lip and fingered the black, leathery teats. 'I wouldn't be surprised,' he said.

'Well, she isn't changed at all. It's three months gone.'

1. A small rodent

Billy rubbed the mare's flat forehead with his knuckle while she grunted with pleasure. 'I told you you'd get tired waiting. It'll be five months more before you can even see a sign, and it'll be at least eight months more before she throws the colt, about next January.'

Jody sighed deeply. 'It's a long time, isn't it?'

'And then it'll be about two years more before you can ride.'

Jody cried out in despair, 'I'll be grown up.'

'Yep, you'll be an old man,' said Billy.

'What colour do you think the colt'll be?'

'Why, you can't ever tell. The stud is black and the dam is bay. Colt might be black or bay or grey or dappled. You can't tell. Sometimes a black dam might have a white colt.'

'Well, I hope it's black, and a stallion.'

'If it's a stallion, we'll have to geld it. Your father wouldn't let you have a stallion.'

'Maybe he would,' Jody said. 'I could train him not to be mean.'

Billy pursed his lips, and the little straw that had been in the corner of his mouth rolled down to the centre. 'You can't ever trust a stallion,' he said critically. 'They're mostly fighting and making trouble. Sometimes when they're feeling funny they won't work. They make the mares uneasy and kick hell out of the geldings. Your father wouldn't let you keep a stallion.'

Nellie sauntered away, nibbling the drying grass. Jody skinned the grain from a grass stem and threw the handful into the air, so that each pointed, feathered seed sailed out like a dart. 'Tell me how it'll be, Billy. Is it like when the cows have calves?'

'Just about. Mares are a little more sensitive. Sometimes you have to be there to help the mare. And sometimes if it's wrong, you have to –' he paused.

'Have to what, Billy?'

'Have to tear the colt to pieces to get it out, or the mare'll die.'

'But it won't be that way this time, will it, Billy?'

'Oh, no. Nellie's thrown good colts.'

'Can I be there, Billy? Will you be certain to call me? It's my colt.'

'Sure, I'll call you. Of course I will.'

'Tell me how it'll be.'

'Why, you've seen the cows calving. It's almost the same. The mare starts groaning and stretching, and then, if it's a good right birth, the head and forefeet come out, and the front hoofs kick a hole just the way the calves do. And the colt starts to breathe. It's good to be there, 'cause if its feet aren't right maybe he can't break the sack, and then he might smother.'

Jody whipped his leg with a bunch of grass. 'We'll have to be there, then, won't we?'

'Oh, we'll be there all right.'

They turned and walked slowly down the hill toward the barn. Jody was tortured with a thing he had to say, although he didn't want to. 'Billy,' he began miserably, 'Billy, you won't let anything happen to the colt, will you?'

And Billy knew he was thinking of the red pony, Gabilan, and of how it had died of strangles. Billy knew he had been infallible before that, and now he was capable of failure. This knowledge made Billy much less sure of himself than he had been. 'I can't tell,' he said roughly. 'All sorts of things might happen, and they wouldn't be my fault. I can't do everything.' He felt badly about his lost prestige, and so he said, meanly, 'I'll do everything I know, but I won't promise anything. Nellie's a good mare. She's thrown good colts before. She ought to this time.' And he walked away from Jody and went into the saddle-room beside the barn, for his feelings were hurt.

Jody travelled often to the brush line behind the house. A rusty iron pipe ran a thin stream of spring water into an old green tub. Where the water spilled over and sank into the ground there was a patch of perpetually green grass. Even when the hills were brown and baked in the summer that little patch was green. The water whined softly into the trough all the year round. This place had grown to be a centre-point for Jody. When he had been punished the cool green grass and the singing water soothed him. When he had been mean the biting acid of meanness left him at the brush line. When he sat in the grass and listened to the purling stream, the barriers set up in his mind by the stern day went down to ruin.

On the other hand, the black cypress tree by the bunk-

house was as repulsive as the water-tub was dear; for to
this tree all the pigs came, sooner or later, to be
slaughtered. Pig-killing was fascinating, with the
screaming and the blood, but it made Jody's heart beat
so fast that it hurt him. After the pigs were scalded in the
big iron tripod kettle and their skins were scraped and
white, Jody had to go to the water-tub to sit in the grass
until his heart grew quiet. The water-tub and the black
cypress were opposites and enemies.

When Billy left him and walked angrily away, Jody
turned up towards the house. He thought of Nellie as he
walked, and of the little colt. Then suddenly he saw that
he was under the black cypress, under the very single-
tree where the pigs were hung. He brushed his dry-grass
hair off his forehead and hurried on. It seemed to him an
unlucky thing to be thinking of his colt in the very
slaughter place, especially after what Billy had said. To
counteract any evil result of that bad conjunction he
walked quickly past the ranch-house, through the
chicken yard, through the vegetable patch, until he came
at last to the brush line.

He sat down in the green grass. The trilling water
sounded in his ears. He looked over the farm buildings
and across at the round hills, rich and yellow with grain.
He could see Nellie feeding on the slope. As usual the
water place eliminated time and distance. Jody saw a
black, long-legged colt, butting against Nellie's flanks,
demanding milk. And then he saw himself breaking a
large colt to halter. All in a few moments the colt grew

to be a magnificent animal, deep of chest, with a neck as high and arched as a sea-horse's neck, with a tail that tongued and rippled like black flame. This horse was terrible to everyone but Jody. In the school yard the boys begged rides, and Jody smilingly agreed. But no sooner were they mounted than the black demon pitched them off. Why, that was his name. Black Demon! For a moment the trilling water and the grass and the sunshine came back, and then . . .

Sometimes in the night the ranch people, safe in their beds, heard a roar of hoofs go by. They said, 'It's Jody, on Demon. He's helping out the sheriff again.' And then . . .

The golden dust filled the air in the arena at Salinas Rodeo. The announcer called the roping contests. When Jody rode the black horse to the starting chute the other contestants shrugged and gave up first place, for it was well known that Jody and Demon could rope and throw and tie a steer a great deal quicker than any roping team of two men could. Jody was not a boy any more, and Demon was not a horse. The two together were one glorious individual. And then . . .

The President wrote a letter and asked them to help catch a bandit in Washington. Jody settled himself comfortably in the grass. The little stream of water whined into the mossy tub.

The year passed slowly on. Time after time Jody gave up his colt for lost. No change had taken place in Nellie.

Carl Tiflin still drove her to a light cart, and she pulled on a hay rake and worked the Jackson-fork tackle when the hay was being put into the barn.

The summer passed, and the warm bright autumn. And then the frantic morning winds began to twist along the ground, and a chill came into the air, and the poison oak turned red. One morning in September, when he had finished his breakfast, Jody's mother called him into the kitchen. She was pouring boiling water into a bucket full of dry middlings and stirring the materials to a steaming paste.

'Yes, ma'am?' Jody asked.

'Watch how I do it. You'll have to do it after this every other morning.'

'Well, what is it?'

'Why, it's warm mash for Nellie. It'll keep her in good shape.'

Jody rubbed his forehead with a knuckle. 'Is she all right?' he asked timidly.

Mrs Tiflin put down the kettle and stirred the mash with a wooden paddle. 'Of course she's all right, only you've got to take better care of her from now on. Here, take this breakfast out to her!'

Jody seized the bucket and ran, down past the bunkhouse, past the barn, with the heavy bucket banging against his knees. He found Nellie playing with the water in the trough, pushing waves and tossing her head so that the water slopped out on the ground.

Jody climbed the fence and set the bucket of steaming

mash beside her. Then he stepped back to look at her. And she was changed. Her stomach was swollen. When she moved, her feet touched the ground gently. She buried her nose in the bucket and gobbled the hot breakfast. And when she had finished and had pushed the bucket around the ground with her nose a little, she stepped quietly over to Jody and rubbed her cheek against him.

Billy Buck came out of the saddle-room and walked over. 'Starts fast when it starts, doesn't it?'

'Did it come all at once?'

'Oh, no, you just stopped looking for a while.' He pulled her head around toward Jody. 'She's goin' to be nice, too. See how nice her eyes are! Some mares turn mean, but when they turn nice, they just love everything.' Nellie slipped her head under Billy's arm and rubbed her neck up and down between his arm and his side. 'You better treat her awful nice now,' Billy said.

'How long will it be?' Jody demanded breathlessly.

The man counted in whispers on his fingers. 'About three months,' he said aloud. 'You can't tell exactly. Sometimes it's eleven months to the day, but it might be two weeks early, or a month late, without hurting anything.'

Jody looked hard at the ground. 'Billy,' he began nervously, 'Billy, you'll call me when it's getting born, won't you? You'll let me be there, won't you?'

Billy bit the tip of Nellie's ear with his front teeth. 'Carl says he wants you to start right at the start. That's the only way to learn. Nobody can tell you anything. Like my old man did with me about the saddle blanket. He was a government packer when I was your size, and I helped him some. One day I left a wrinkle in my saddle blanket and made a saddle-sore. My old man didn't give me hell at all. But the next morning he saddled me up with a forty-pound stock saddle. I had to lead my horse and carry that saddle over a whole damn mountain in the sun. It darn near killed me, but I never left no wrinkles in a blanket again. I couldn't. I never in my life since then put on a blanket but I felt that saddle on my back.'

Jody reached up a hand and took hold of Nellie's mane. 'You'll tell me what to do about everything, won't you? I guess you know everything about horses, don't you?'

Billy laughed. 'Why I'm half horse myself, you see,' he said. 'My ma died when I was born, and being my old man was a government packer in the mountains, and no cows around most of the time, why he just gave me mostly mare's milk.' He continued seriously. 'And horses know that. Don't you know it, Nellie?'

The mare turned her head and looked full into his eyes for a moment, and this is a thing horses practically never do. Billy was proud and sure of himself now. He boasted a little. 'I'll see you get a good colt. I'll start you right. And if you do like I say, you'll have the best horse in the country.'

That made Jody feel warm and proud, too; so proud

that when he went back to the house he bowed his legs and swayed his shoulders as horsemen do. And he whispered, 'Whoa, you Black Demon, you! Steady down there and keep your feet on the ground.'

The winter fell sharply. A few preliminary gusty showers, and then a strong steady rain. The hills lost their straw colour and blackened under the water, and the winter streams scrambled noisily down the canyons. The mushrooms and puffballs popped up and the new grass started before Christmas.

But this year Christmas was not the central day to Jody. Some undetermined time in January had become the axis day around which the months swung. When the rains fell, he put Nellie in a box stall and fed her warm food every morning and curried her and brushed her.

The mare was swelling so greatly that Jody became alarmed. 'She'll pop wide open,' he said to Billy.

Billy laid his strong square hand against Nellie's swollen abdomen. 'Feel here,' he said quietly. 'You can feel it move. I guess it would surprise you if there were twin colts.'

'You don't think so?' Jody cried. 'You don't think it will be twins, do you, Billy?'

'No, I don't, but it does happen, sometimes.'

During the first two weeks of January it rained steadily. Jody spent most of his time, when he wasn't in school, in the box stall with Nellie. Twenty times a day he put his hand on her stomach to feel the colt move. Nellie became more and more gentle and friendly to him. She rubbed her nose on him. She whinnied softly when he walked into the barn.

Carl Tiflin came to the barn with Jody one day. He looked admiringly at the groomed bay coat, and he felt the firm flesh over ribs and shoulders. 'You've done a good job,' he said to Jody. And this was the greatest praise he knew how to give. Jody was tight with pride for hours afterward.

The fifteenth of January came, and the colt was not born. And the twentieth came; a lump of fear began to form in Jody's stomach. 'Is it all right?' he demanded of Billy.

'Oh, sure.'

And again: 'Are you sure it's going to be all right?'

Billy stroked the mare's neck. She swayed her head uneasily. 'I told you it wasn't always the same time, Jody. You just have to wait.'

When the end of the month arrived with no birth, Jody grew frantic. Nellie was so big that her breath came heavily, and her ears were close together and straight up, as though her head ached. Jody's sleep grew restless and his dreams confused.

On the night of the second of February he awakened crying. His mother called to him, 'Jody, you're dreaming. Wake up and start over again.'

But Jody was filled with terror and desolation. He lay quietly a few moments, waiting for his mother to go back to sleep, and then he slipped his clothes on, and crept out in his bare feet.

The night was black and thick. A little misting rain fell. The cypress tree and the bunk-house loomed and then dropped back into the mist. The barn door screeched as he opened it, a thing it never did in the daytime. Jody went to the rack and found a lantern and a tin box of matches. He lighted the wick and walked down the long straw-covered aisle to Nellie's stall. She was standing up. Her whole body weaved from side to side. Jody called to her, 'So, Nellie, so-o, Nellie,' but she did not stop her swaying nor look around. When he stepped into the stall and touched her on the shoulder she shivered under his hand. Then Billy Buck's voice came from the hayloft right above the stall.

'Jody, what are you doing?'

Jody started back and turned miserable eyes up toward the nest where Billy was lying in the hay. 'Is she all right, do you think?'

'Why sure, I think so.'

'You won't let anything happen, Billy, you're sure you won't?'

Billy growled down at him, 'I told you I'd call you, and I will. Now you get back to bed and stop worrying that mare. She's got enough to do without you worrying her.'

Jody cringed, for he had never heard Billy speak in such a tone. 'I only thought I'd come and see,' he said. 'I woke up.'

Billy softened a little then. 'Well, you get to bed. I don't want you bothering her. I told you I'd get you a good colt. Get along now.'

Jody walked slowly out of the barn. He blew out the lantern and set it in the rack. The blackness of the night, and the chilled mist struck him and enfolded him. He wished he believed everything Billy said as he had before the pony died. It was a moment before his eyes, blinded by the feeble lantern-flame, could make any form of the darkness. The damp ground chilled his bare feet. At the cypress tree the roosting turkeys chattered a little in alarm, and the two good dogs responded to their duty and came charging out, barking to frighten away the coyotes they thought were prowling under the tree.

As he crept through the kitchen, Jody stumbled over a chair. Carl called from his bedroom, 'Who's there? What's the matter there?'

And Mrs Tiflin said sleepily, 'What's the matter, Carl?'

The next second Carl came out of the bedroom carrying a candle, and found Jody before he could get into bed. 'What are you doing out?'

Jody turned shyly away. 'I was down to see the mare.'

For a moment anger at being awakened fought with approval in Jody's father. 'Listen,' he said, finally, 'there's not a man in this country that knows more about colts than Billy. You leave it to him.'

Words burst out of Jody's mouth, 'But the pony died —'

'Don't you go blaming that on him,' Carl said sternly. 'If Billy can't save a horse, it can't be saved.'

Mrs Tiflin called, 'Make him clean his feet and go to bed, Carl. He'll be sleepy all day to-morrow.'

It seemed to Jody that he had just closed his eyes to try to go to sleep when he was shaken violently by the shoulder. Billy Buck stood beside him, holding a lantern in his hand. 'Get up,' he said. 'Hurry up.' He turned and walked quickly out of the room.

Mrs Tiflin called, 'What's the matter? Is that you, Billy?'

'Yes, ma'am.'

'Is Nellie ready?'

'Yes, ma'am.'

'All right, I'll get up and heat some water in case you need it.'

Jody jumped into his clothes so quickly that he was out the back door before Billy's swinging lantern was halfway to the barn. There was a rim of dawn on the mountain-tops, but no light had penetrated into the cup of the ranch yet. Jody ran frantically after the lantern and caught up to Billy just as he reached the barn. Billy hung the lantern to a nail on the stall-side and took off his blue denim coat. Jody saw that he wore only a sleeveless shirt under it.

Nellie was standing rigid and stiff. While they watched, she crouched. Her whole body was wrung with a spasm. The spasm passed. But in a few moments it started over again, and passed.

Billy muttered nervously, 'There's something wrong.' His bare hand disappeared. 'Oh, God,' he said. 'It's wrong.'

The spasm came again, and this time Billy strained, and the muscles stood out on his arm and shoulder. He

heaved strongly, his forehead beaded with perspiration. Nellie cried with pain. Billy was muttering, 'It's wrong. I can't turn it. It's way wrong. It's turned all around wrong.'

He glared wildly toward Jody. And then his fingers made a careful, careful diagnosis. His cheeks were growing tight and grey. He looked for a long questioning minute at Jody standing back of the stall. Then Billy stepped to the rack under the manure window and picked up a horseshoe hammer with his wet right hand.

'Go outside, Jody,' he said.

The boy stood still and stared dully at him.

'Go outside, I tell you. It'll be too late.'

Jody didn't move.

Then Billy walked quickly to Nellie's head. He cried, 'Turn your face away, damn you, turn your face.'

This time Jody obeyed. His head turned sideways. He heard Billy whispering hoarsely in the stall. And then he heard a hollow crunch of bone. Nellie chuckled shrilly. Jody looked back in time to see the hammer rise and fall again on the flat forehead. Then Nellie fell heavily to her side and quivered for a moment.

Billy jumped to the swollen stomach; his big pocket-knife was in his hand. He lifted the skin and drove the knife in.

Billy dropped the knife. Both of his arms plunged in and dragged out a big, white, dripping bundle. His teeth tore a hole in the covering. A little black head appeared through the tear, and little slick, wet ears. A

gurgling breath was drawn, and then another. Billy
shucked off the sac and found his knife and cut the string.
For a moment he held the little black colt in his arms and
looked at it. And then he walked slowly over and laid it
in the straw at Jody's feet.

Billy's face and arms and chest were dripping red. His
body shivered and his teeth chattered. His voice was
gone; he spoke in a throaty whisper: 'There's your colt.
I promised. And there it is. I had to do it – had to.' He
stopped and looked over his shoulder into the box stall.

'Go get hot water and a sponge,' he whispered. 'Wash him and dry him the way his mother would. You'll have to feed him by hand. But there's your colt, the way I promised.'

Jody stared stupidly at the wet, panting foal. It stretched out its chin and tried to raise its head. Its blank eyes were navy-blue.

'God damn you,' Billy shouted, 'will you go now for the water? *Will* you go?'

Then Jody turned and trotted out of the barn into the dawn. He ached from his throat to his stomach. His legs were stiff and heavy. He tried to be glad because of the colt, but the bloody face and the haunted, tired eyes of Billy Buck hung in the air ahead of him.

TITLES IN THE NEW WINDMILL SERIES

Chinua Achebe: *Things Fall Apart*
Louisa M. Alcott: *Little Women*
Elizabeth Allen: *Deitz and Denny*
Eric Allen: *The Latchkey Children*
Bernard Ashley: *A Kind of Wild Justice; High Pavement Blues; Running Scared*
Enid Bagnold: *National Velvet*
Martin Ballard: *Dockie*
Stan Barstow: *Joby*
Nina Bawden: *On the Run; The Witch's Daughter; A Handful of Thieves; Carrie's War;*
  Rebel on a Rock; The Robbers; Devil by the Sea, Kept in the Dark
Rex Benedict: *Last Stand at Goodbye Gulch*
Paul Berna: *Flood Warning*
Judy Blume: *It's Not the End of the World; Tiger Eyes*
Pierre Boulle: *The Bridge on the River Kwai*
E. R. Braithwaite: *To Sir, With Love*
F. Hodgson Burnett: *The Secret Garden*
Helen Bush: *Mary Anning's Treasures*
Betsy Byars: *The Midnight Fox*
John Caldwell: *Desperate Voyage*
Albert Camus: *The Outsider*
Victor Canning: *The Runaways; Flight of the Grey Goose*
Charles Chaplin: *My Early Years*
John Christopher: *The Guardians; Empty World*
Richard Church: *The Cave; Over the Bridge*
Colette: *My Mother's House*
Alexander Cordell: *The Traitor Within*
Margaret Craven: *I Heard the Owl Call my Name*
Roald Dahl: *Danny, The Champion of the World; The Wonderful Story of Henry Sugar;*
  George's Marvellous Medicine; The BFG; The Witches; Boy
Andrew Davies: *Conrad's War*
Anita Desai: *The Village by the Sea*
Meindert de Jong: *The Wheel on the School*
Peter Dickinson: *The Gift; Annerton Pit; Healer*
Eleanor Doorly: *The Radium Woman*
Gerald Durrell: *Three Singles to Adventure; The Drunken Forest*
Malcolm Edwards (Editor): *Constellations*
Elizabeth Enright: *The Saturdays*
J. M. Falkner: *Moonfleet*
Anne Fine: *The Granny Project*
F. Scott Fitzgerald: *The Great Gatsby*
Jane Gardam: *The Hollow Land*
Leon Garfield: *Six Apprentices*
Eve Garnett: *The Family from One End Street; Further Adventures of the Family from One End*
  Street
G. M. Glaskin: *A Waltz through the Hills*
Rumer Godden: *Black Narcissus*
Kenneth Grahame: *The Wind in the Willows*
Graham Greene: *The Third Man* and *The Fallen Idol; The Power and The Glory; Brighton*
  Rock
John Griffin: *Skulker Wheat; The Fight and Other Stories*
René Guillot: *Kpo the Leopard*
Thomas Hardy: *The Withered Arm and Other Wessex Tales*
Rosemary Harris: *Zed*
Ann Harries: *The Sound of the Gora*
L. P. Hartley: *The Go-Between*
Jan De Hartog: *The Lost Sea*
Erik Haugaard: *The Little Fishes*

Esther Hautzig: *The Endless Steppe*
Ernest Hemingway: *The Old Man and the Sea ; A Farewell to Arms*
John Hersey: *A Single Pebble*
Nigel Hinton: *Getting Free; Buddy*
Alfred Hitchcock: *Sinister Spies*
Russell Hoban: *The Mouse and his Child*
C. Walter Hodges: *The Overland Launch*
Richard Hough: *Razor Eyes*
Geoffrey Household: *Rogue Male ; Escape into Daylight*
Janni Howker: *Badger on the Barge*
Monica Hughes: *Ring-Rise, Ring-Set*
Shirley Hughes: *Here Comes Charlie Moon ; Charlie Moon and the Big Bonanza Bust-Up*
Barbara Ireson (Editor) : *In a Class of Their Own*
Jennifer Johnson: *Shadows on Our Skin*
Toeckey Jones: *Go Well, Stay Well*
James Joyce: *A Portrait of the Artist as a Young Man*
Josephine Kamm: *Young Mother; Out of Step; Where Do We Go From Here?; The Starting Point*
Erich Kästner: *Emil and the Detectives; Lottie and Lisa*
Geraldine Kaye: *Comfort Herself*
M. E. Kerr: *Dinky Hocker Shoots Smack!; Gentlehands*
Clive King: *Me and My Million*
Dick King-Smith: *The Sheep-Pig*
John Knowles: *A Separate Peace*
Marghanita Laski: *Little Boy Lost*
D. H. Lawrence: *Sea and Sardinia; The Fox* and *The Virgin and the Gypsy; Selected Tales*
Harper Lee: *To Kill a Mockingbird*
Laurie Lee: *As I Walked Out One Midsummer Morning*
Ursula Le Guin: *A Wizard of Earthsea ; A Very Long Way from Anywhere Else*
C. Day Lewis: *The Otterbury Incident*
Lorna Lewis: *Leonardo the Inventor*
Martin Lindsay: *The Epic of Captain Scott*
David Line: *Run for Your Life ; Mike and Me ; Under Plum Lake ; Screaming High*
Kathleen Lines: *The House of the Nightmare*
Joan Lingard: *Across the Barricades; Into Exile; The Clearance; The File on Fräulein Berg*
Penelope Lively: *The Ghost of Thomas Kempe*
Jack London: *The Call of the Wild; White Fang*
Carson McCullers: *The Member of the Wedding*
Margaret Mahy: *The Haunting ; The Catalogue of The Universe*
Wolf Mankowitz: *A Kid for Two Farthings*
Jan Mark: *Thunder and Lightnings; Under the Autumn Garden*
James Vance Marshall: *A River Ran Out of Eden; Walkabout; My Boy John that Went to Sea; A Walk to the Hills of the Dreamtime*
David Martin: *The Cabby's Daughter*
W. Somerset Maugham: *The Kite and Other Stories*
Guy de Maupassant: *Prisoners of War and Other Stories*
William Mayne: *Drift*
Yvonne Mitchell: *Cathy Away*
Honoré Morrow: *The Splendid Journey*
R. K. Narayan: *A Tiger for Malgudi*
Bill Naughton: *The Goalkeeper's Revenge; A Dog Called Nelson; My Pal Spadger*
E. Nesbit: *The Railway Children; The Story of the Treasure Seekers*
Emily Neville: *It's Like this, Cat*
Mary Norton: *The Borrowers*
Christine Nostlinger: *Conrad the Factory-Made Boy*
Robert C. O'Brien: *Mrs Frisby and the Rats of NIMH; Z for Zachariah*
Scott O'Dell: *Island of the Blue Dolphins*